A PLACE IN THE SHADOWS

Find Your Light

Matthew Hernandez

I dedicate this book to my beautiful partner Sophie Hernandez and my amazing daughter Gabriella Hernandez. You have both supported me throughout the process of writing this book and never gave up on me, so thank you, I love you, and this ones for you.

CONTENTS

Title Page

Copyright

Dedication

Chapter 1: My Life   1

Chapter 2: Unexpected Visitor   23

Chapter 3: A Place In The Shadows   33

Chapter 4: The Transition   41

Chapter 5: Who Am I?   58

Chapter 6: Hunted   68

Chapter 7: You've Made It Personal   78

Chapter 8: Trapped   90

Chapter 9: From Hunter To Hunted   100

Chapter 10: Not Alone   119

CHAPTER 1 : MY LIFE

The large droplets of rain pattered against the glass of the thin single glazed windows with a melodic vibe just loud enough to drown out the chatter back and forth from the students which filled the room with a resounding buzz. Mr Baldwick, a short old aged teacher stood statuesque at the front of the class explaining the theory of trigonometry with a joyous enthusiasm that only a maths teacher could possess, that did all but grasp the attention of the 16 year old audience who continued with their own personal discussions.

"Max Baxter, do I have your attention" yelled Mr Baldwick whose wrinkles bulged, becoming ever more potent as he frowned across the room. "Yes Sir, I was just daydreaming" answered a quiet voice from the furthest back seat in the corner of the room. The voice came from a timid looking, skinny, small statured teenager. His jet black hair was unkept, messy and swept across his face so as to reveal only a small portion of his pale complexity to be on display to the world.

Sniggers and giggles echoed throughout the classroom as his fellow students mocked his innocence, seeming to maliciously thrive on the punishment of what seemed like an already unconfident person. "Very well" spoke Mr Baldwick reluctantly before continuing his rant about the wonderful genius of trigonometry to his bewildered class.

"Well done four eyes, why are you even alive?" spoke a deep voice from the table beside him, followed by the giggles of the popular girls surrounding him. The voice belonged to a large muscular framed jock beside him, whose blonde hair, blue eyes and undeniable confidence glowed from his cocky nature. "Just piss off James!" yelled Max in an unfiltered, rage filled spurt, wishing he could now swallow the words that had just left his lips.

"Mr Baxter, Headmasters office immediately!" bellowed the small teacher who finally had the full attention of the class and was clearly angered for once again having to pause in his presentation. Max rose slowly from his seat slumping forwards, clearly embarrassed for the attention he now had placed on himself, turning only to grab his Black blazer and bag situated on the back of his seat.

"You are a dead man" whispered James, clearly loud enough for only the Max to hear, the rage pertinent in his eyes as he stared with a writhing hatred towards Max who didn't dare lock eyes with him. Heading through the rows of tables towards the door Max could only focus on one thing; the threat ringing repeatedly in his mind, anxious of the future punishment he will now be subject to as a result for his outburst. Max was so absorbed in his consequential thoughts that he didn't even notice how heads turned as he passed through the rows of tables toward the exit, each student gazing at him in sheer amazement for piping up to the hardest person in school.

"Well done Max, you really are a genius, congrats on painting an even larger red target board on your back, he's gonna get me afterschool" he thought to himself as he navigated sluggishly through the high ceilinged rustic empty hallways on route to the headmasters office. Shaking from the fear running through his body, Max raises his hand to knock tepidly on the door to the headmasters office. "Come in" spoke a deep but soft voice, Max proceeded to enter the large oval shaped office which consisted of built in bookcases and a soft plush carpet unseen in any other room in the school. In the centre of the office sat a middle-aged, dark haired bearded man dressed both smart and casually, with a welcoming smile.

He slowly closes the lid of his laptop whilst peering over his glasses to get a better look at small scruffy teenager stood before him, "how is it I can help you today?" he asked softly, reassuring Max that the fear of James is vastly larger than the fear he has of his principal. "S-sorry to bother you sir, I-I've been sent to you by Mr Baldwin" timidly spoke Max whose words quietly left his lips ashamedly as he re-lived this memory once again in his mind.

Changing his composure to an almost upright position, the headmaster's eyes narrowed, his persona of niceties was lost and the gravity of the situation was now portrayed through the aggressively diplomatic expression on his face. "And why is it you have been sent to me?!" the headmaster sternly spoke, his voice no longer containing the soft quality it previously held. Max continued to stand nervously by the door and explained the scenario of what had happened.

"Come and take a seat" the headteacher Mr Phillips demanded, "Regardless of the aggression you felt at that moment in time, lashing out with foul language will not resolve the problem only further evoke that you are in the wrong." spoke Mr Phillips. The severity in his voice and body language seemed to dim down like the dimming of a light, leaving only a calm and authoritative composure sat opposite the much younger Max, who he saw a similar reflection of his childhood self within.

"Being bullied is a painful and sensitive experience, with which few can realise the emotional trauma experienced at the time, I went through it as a child and suffered severely at the hands of those who at the time I cowered before. But fear and just accepting all that is wrong because society and social norms specify your place in the hierarchy is a load of rubbish. Don't be oppressed anymore, I should not say this but; fight back, show them that you are in fact more of a man than they are and then Max anything will be possible" spoke Mr Phillips once again softly preaching and sharing his personal experience with the overwhelmed Max who now sat speechless before him.

An awkward but relaxing silence as Max pondered over the advice he was given filled the space with a blank aura of intimate meditative peace. "Thanks Sir, but I'm fine, honest. Sorry for my outburst I will make sure it won't happen again" said Max standing up from his seat and heading towards the door of the office. His feelings of pain and despair within himself bubbling as he continues to hate school because of the way in which he is actively bullied and humiliated, he couldn't bring himself to release the lid of the emotional bottle contained inside him. The rest of the day continued as a blur, Max avoided open empty spaces at all costs, fearing James might spontaneously materialise from the vast emptiness to punish him for his previous mistake.

The clock relentlessly ticked for what felt like an eternity until at 15:15 the bell rang to signal the end of the final class of the day for all students. The part of the day Max had been fearing most, "Should I stay late and hope he doesn't find me, or should I run home?" his inner dialogue ran endlessly with every possible outcome to avoid bumping into James however improbable this may be. He left the school grounds unhindered and turned into the alleyway through to his house.

"Max! There you are Mr predictable, thought you would get away" James said almost cackling as he did. He stood there around 6 foot tall puffed up with two friends standing behind him. "I-I didn't mean it James mate honest" begged Max with a pure sincerity as James paced towards him. "I'm not your mate!" yelled James throwing his fist at Max, the crunch was audible to even his friends who grimaced as Max fell backwards, his head whipping back as the force of the punch takes his centre of gravity from him. The warm sensation tingles in his cheek as his ears begin to ring, and the weight of his frail body crashes into the ground. Standing over him he sees the outline of James' large build, raising his foot up before thrusting it towards Max's face whose eyesight fades to blackness.

"Can you hear me? Max can you hear me?" A concerned female voice quizzed him repeatedly, his senses began to come back, the noise of footsteps moving around him, the cold sensation of oxygen filling his lungs, the iron like taste of blood, the aches and sensations of his body and face. "Max, sweetheart please, please respond" spoke a panicked female voice, her words almost not understandable through her loud sobs, he recognises this voice to be his mothers. Raising his hand he mumbles "mum" and slowly attempts to open his eyes, the swelling making this a near impossible feat where only a squint is possible. The bright light burning into his eyes somewhat blinding him, from the light of the doctor's torch.

"Max, you are in A&E, you have been jumped and we just need to run some checks and help you to recover." spoke the young sounding nurse, her voice tenderly filled with genuine empathy. "Mum..." he mumbled again, this time his words barely managing to escape his mouth. "His heart rate is dropping! Give me 50mg of Cordarone, beginning CPR" yelled the doctor in a frenzied panic.

"Hi Max, how are you feeling son?" spoke the soft but excited voice of his mother. Max heard her voice gently waking him as he turned to face her, opening his eyes now with ease to see a blurry focus of his mother who sat beside him. His mother was a short, slightly overweight woman whose short brown hair was curled into perfect ringlets, she was wearing a summery flowered dress and clutched her magazine as if it were the life source of her sanity.

"I remember James, and then here and I heard your voice?" asked Max curious as to how it was possible for his rapid change of health . "Max my love, they placed you into a chemically induced coma to allow your body to focus on physically healing itself and allow your mind to rest. It has been 12 days son, but you look so much better, I promise" She said her sincerity, blatantly obvious as the tear ran down her face, "I was so worried..." she continued before bursting into tears of relief. "For now, just rest, we are here whenever you need us Max, we love you" spoke his mum as she rose to her feet and ushered his little sister from the room who he had not noticed.

Days passed, Max's face and body continued to heal, his energy levels rising until he was able to coherently hold a conversation without a lack of words and tiring at the thought of memories. Through this time the incident slowly came back to him, piece by piece, all part of something bigger, the jigsaw of his injuries, and the crippling memory of his pain.

"Good afternoon Mr Baxter, we were wondering if we could ask you a few questions" asked a formally dressed police officer, he was a large man situated over 6 foot with a muscular build and a face that whilst now showing the utmost sympathy was undeniably capable of portraying power and authority. "Hi" said Max once again timid and unsure of what to do; Does he tell what he remembers? Will they get him worse? What should he do? What is the right thing to do? This flurry of questions passed instantaneously through his mind so fast that he hadn't time to answer one before the next question was asked.

"I understand that you are most likely feeling confused and anxious with the incident, it is a common symptom for victims, but trust me lad, I only want to do what is best for you... A kind man saved your life, he witnessed three similar aged individuals kicking you whilst on the floor, he shouted and they ran, he then called 999 for you. Can you remember this? Do you know who they were?" the policeman spoke with a reassuring tone as if to gain Max's trust however couldn't have been further from the truth.

"If I'm honest sir, I don't really remember what happened. I went to school and on the way home someone jumped me. I just remember everything went black" Max explained as if exacerbated by attempting to conjure back the dreadful memory that resulted in his current physical condition. "No worries Mr Baxter we apologise for what you have gone through, we shall continue to investigate but if you do remember anything at all please do not hesitate to contact me" and with that comment he passed Max his card with all of his details before striding out of the room.

Max spent the rest of that day staring at the card, pondering whether to contact the officer and confirm what actually happened that day. But indecisiveness consumed his mind and his indecision led to an inaction that ultimately decided for him. Later that night Max is woken by a voice "Oi Max" spoke a familiar deep voice startling Max as he woke unexpectedly. "You best not have told anyone what happened you little dweeb! Otherwise next time we won't stop" threatened the voice with a deadly calm that evoked the seriousness of the words spoken. "No James I haven't told anyone, and I promise this will never happen to me again you sick twisted bully" spoke Max who rose slowly in his bed, locking eyes with James in a desperate attempt to prove his newfound lack of fear. "I'll be the judge of that you pussy!" grunted James before pacing from the room, double checking that no-one saw him enter or leave. Max sighed a breath of relief and a lion-like sense of pride rushed over his body as he had finally confronted his fear with pure poise. He rested his head back against the soft cushion of the hospital imagining his future and his ability to defend himself.

Max always had an astounding imagination he could become captured in a thought so resounding through his mind he would drift into the alternate universe it created. He spent the rest of the week dreaming and visualising his defeat of his seemingly undefeatable foe, but if David can beat Goliath, then I can beat him, he kept repeating to himself. These continued as he began his favourite pastime; reading where he could further escape the unequitable struggles of mundane life from the glorious fantasy of fiction and his absorption within the pages.

The rest of the week flew by and Max inadvertently felt positive and excited to be leaving the room to which he was confined and step back into the real world. The rush he felt when first stepping out of the hospital, his senses were overwhelmed, the bright light of the sun reflecting off of every object into his pupils, the brush of a soft wind pressing lightly against his skin and the chatter of those around him, each person following their own unique monologue, Max had a new appreciation for life. He was accompanied out of the hospital by his mother who continued to nurture him as if still in the critical condition he initially was in. "Come on Max let's get you home" she spoke softly, opening the car door for him as if his arms were no longer able to manage the task. He gratefully enters the vehicle and they head home.

Only one moment, captured in a single glance as he turned his head, stood out on route to his home 'Briggs MMA'. The sign hung above a rustic warehouse with rolling doors at the front, the red letters tainted by the sunlight cracking the wood of the sign beneath the paint. Fear but determination burned inside Max has he debated whether to try attending the gym to give it a go, the fear was induced by the anxiety of the unknown and not being able to contemplate what to expect, whilst his determination thrived from the inner belief that he will never allow this to happen to himself again. "I will be prepared for the future, I need to learn to hold my own" he spoke to himself, the inadequate but surprisingly helpful inner pep talk, and with that Max changed into his trainers, tracksuit bottoms, unused for years, and a moderately white but stained tank top and headed out the door.

"1, 2, 3 and under" screamed a voice in a military

styled fashion as he entered Briggs MMA warehouse. The open space was filled in a mist like fashion with the musky scent of sweat, the only sounds consisted of grunts, heavy breathing and smashes as men ruthlessly beat the punch bags hung from the ceiling by chains. Multiple trainers were in the room, easily distinguishable by the branded companies t-shirts worn by them, 3 separate groups were running, one following a circuit, the other beating the bags, and the final practising technique with walk a through followed by sparring. Green mats were spread across the floor and sweat/blood stains were present, Max instantly questioned his decision and was about to pivot and turn out of the room when a friendly voice greeted him "Hi there" said a slim toned man wearing UFC gear.

"My name's Jack Briggs, how can I help you today? You wanna train kid?" the man spoke, stunning Max with his outgoing friendly composure but rough exterior image. "Y-yes, please sir" Max almost whispered, cowering as the realisation of the situation he had just placed himself in, came to light. "What's your name kid?" Jack spoke, his question still filled with a mild enthusiasm for seeing a new face. "Max sir" he responded, "Oh I'm no sir Max, trust me. You're not the usual sort of person to pop in here, what pushed you to come here?" questioned Jack with genuine interest for the motives behind the small statured, skinny framed boy standing before him.

Max thought for a moment searching inside himself for a genuine reason, as all reasons to stay had left his mind after the intimidating experience of stepping into the gym. "I-I guess, I wanna be able to defend myself," Max said, his head still tilted down to the floor and his eyes covered by the hair he had brushed across his face prior to entering. "Well that's as good of a reason as any, just make sure you find that fire inside that truly drives you, because without that unforgiving drive to push you through your pain barriers into new unimaginable realms, you will need a core motive, just remember that kid" spoke Jack with a mature wisdom clearly gained through personal experience.

Max removed his shoes as requested by Jack before following him into the small office situated in the rear corner of the room. Max signed a disclaimer and made his first payment before heading out into the gym. "You start with circuits to warm up, then pads and bags and finish with technique and sparring, let's see what you've got" Jack spoke pointing towards the tall large framed muscular trainer leading the circuit route.

"Move, move, move! Come on kid" yelled the trainer eagerly, Max ran across the mats towards the circuit route, "start with burpees, follow them and try to keep up kid" spoke the trainer mildly grinning at the questionable expression written on Max's face. Max begins to follow the others, their speed and power undeniably more than his own, he drops to his hands, does a push up and rises to his feet before exploding upwards into a high jump tucking his knees into his chest as he did this. After seven Max's body began to struggle, the rigorous exercise not adapting well to his recently discharged body, in fact he questioned whether before the incident he could have even continued. "Push kid, push!" screamed the trainer in his face, the spray of saliva projecting into Max's face which was unnoticeable due to the quantity of sweat pouring from his forehead.

"Time... now everyone move clockwise to the next exercise!" yelled the instructor. "Oh great" thought Max as he attempted lifting a twelve kilogram kettlebell, his muscles straining as his skinny stature struggled to bear the load of the metal weight gripped with white knuckle tightness in his palm. Swing after swing for what felt like an eternity Max continued to thrust the kettlebell weight high above his head before allowing it to drop and swing back between his legs to start the process again. Every swing took more effort, his shoulders were burning more and more with each agonising rep, his face was red from exertion and the previous irritating feeling of sweat trickling down his neck was now a refreshing treat which he now longed for.

Max continued to follow the circuit, his will power dropping with each exercise switch that occurred. His arms excruciatingly burning, the lactic acid pulsing through each and every muscle in his body most of which he didn't even know he had. Sweat ran like an unrelenting waterfall down his forehead, his breath was shallow and quick, his body beginning to fail due to the strenuous activity. He pressed down for one more push up his arms shaking tenaciously refusing to strain once more, succumbing to the strain the weight of his limp body pressed on them. His trainer dropped to his knees glaring ferociously at the near defeated kid before him, "Don't you drop, don't you bloody dare! You push! Push kid!" he screamed at Max.

The clarity of Jack's earlier statement once again revealing itself in his mind, "what's my motive, my reason, why should I push?" Max asked himself continually, searching his soul for an answer, which it delivered, a mental image of James rose in his mind and as the picture rose so too did the fire inside him, he rose cm by cm screaming with anger as he did so until he reached the top of his push up. "Time" yelled the trainer, rising to his feet with a proud, smug look stretched across his face. Max collapsed face down onto the mats, more relieved than he thought was humanly possible, the image of James still burnt clearly into his mind and he rolled onto his back before sitting up to see the look on his trainers face.

Jack walked across the gym towards Max with an expressionless look towards him. "So kid... congrats on completing the warm-up" he said extending his arm out to offer pulling Max up from the ground, his blank face turning into a distinct smile cheek to cheek. "What?!" questioned Max exacerbated and confused with a worried expression on his face. "Game on kid, game on" said Jack before walking back to his office.

The next morning Max's alarm clock woke him at 8:30am the blur of last night ingrained in his mind, he pondered on the activities, the training, the feeling of self-confidence surging through his body the same way electricity surges through the power mains. "Time to get up" shouted his mum from the kitchen, Max attempted to sit upright, instantly realising the reluctance of his body to comply with such a simple request. Every muscle in his body ached, hesitantly twitching as every brain signal sent to them fell upon deaf ears in such a way he felt mildly paralysed. "Come on Max, it's your first day back, hurry up!" she yelled again, shaking his body out of its temporary frozen state. "Ok mum I'm just coming" Max replied before getting ready for his school day.

As expected, no-one really noticed his return to school, no welcoming gifts or pleasantries Max just faded into the background once again. His day went slowly, he anxiously anticipated how he would feel when he saw James and his friends but fortunately between his timetable and a pure shot of pot luck he managed to avoid that scenario for the whole day. For the next month almost religiously Max trained at Rigby's MMA for an hour and a half every day after school. He finally started to notice he was stronger, faster and had better reflexes than ever before, his improvement was drastic and with it his self-confidence fluctuated forwards finally granting him the permission to hold his head high when walking the halls of the school. Much to Max's surprise, James didn't pay much bother to Max since his arrival back at school, the odd comment here and there, but nothing compared to before.

"Time to make a man from a maggot Max, give it more!" bellowed Jack from the edge of the octagon cage, Max and Pete were sparring ruthlessly, full contact, in fact it was more of a fight than any spar should be. Max and Pete, a new starter to the gym shortly after Max, had been competitively driven to surpass each other's abilities since his arrival. This competitive relationship in turn would motivate the other to further push on and improve themselves. Max was being dominated by Pete, who endlessly threw punches, kicks, knees and elbows at Max who was allowing him to control the rhythm of the fight.

"Move Max, move!" Jack once again called as Max is thrown against the side of the cage and beat on by Pete, each gloved punch smashing into either his face or ribs leaving him dazed and breathless, Max throws a wild punch with all of body weight in it as a last ditch effort filled with the despair of his sense of vulnerability. Pete parries this punch grasping Max's wrist and using his momentum along with his own strength to lift Max up and over his back throwing him with a huge force into the canvas below which did all but soften the landing.

After quickly rising to his feet Pete stands towering over Max who lays defencelessly with his back on the canvas looking helplessly up at his competitor. Pete lifts his foot ready to finish off Max with one final kick. Time seems to stop as déjà vu presents itself to Max who becomes unable to distinguish between the competitor in this moment and James in his past, the surge of sadness and vulnerability is singed by the blazing inferno of rage erupting from the depths of his inner self engulfing everything in the moment pumping an irrefutable amount of adrenaline into every single muscle in his body.

Pete's foot comes crashing down on the canvas with such force the ripple of force spread through the ring, Max however wasn't there, he had rolled to the side just clear enough to see the foot land next to his face. Rolling up onto his feet Max takes his opportunity on the startled Pete and lands an elbow straight in his temple with such vigour that Pete is instantly rendered unconscious and his limp body collapses uncontrollably into the canvas. The fire still burning inside Max's head he raises his foot to throw the final blow he had almost encountered, his body shaking relentlessly, every ounce of his rage demanding he plummet his foot with all of his force.

Gasping for one last breath of air before ending the fight in its entirety, Max's blurred vision seen through the red mist of rage clears just enough to prevent him from finishing his attack, instead slowly lowering his foot back to the canvas and dropping to his knees alongside Pete raising his head gently slapping his face as too wake him up from deep unconscious sleep he had been forced into. "Pete I'm sorry, I'm so so sorry, wake up bud, come on" pleaded Max as Jack jumped into the ring to check on Pete, who slowly began to come back around.

After Pete had been picked up by his mother, sent with an ice pack and packet of paracetamol, Jack called the shaken Max into the office. "What the bloody hell happened?! He was beat, we do NOT hit an unconscious opponent!" yelled Jack sternly, further shaking the already emotionally fragile Max. "I-I lost control, it wasn't me anymore or Pete, I saw James and just wanted to punish and hurt him... like he hurt me!" answered Max clearly still fragile about the scenario as he struggles to choke back the tears, "It almost happened again! But it was me... this time it was me" whispered Max, his words shrouded with shame as he can no longer swallow back the overwhelming emotion and bursts uncontrollably into tears.

Jack looked utterly shocked and confused at this reaction, which he had never before experienced in his gym. "Kid, just remember who you are, you can be as good as you choose, each of us has our own light and darkness, make sure you have the choice! You must choose who you want to be, and never stray from that path." Jack endearingly spoke. "But Max, you can't train here anymore. You need to be able to control your emotions before risking the wellbeing of my other students, I am truly sorry, you will be missed" said Jack sincerely. Max slowly rose from his seat, crippled by the news and left the gym still sobbing as he exited.

Staring out across the city view from his local vantage point Max continued to cry, his mixed emotions of upset and rage swirling like a tornado of borderline schizophrenic uncertainty each emotion fighting to be the more dominant of the two. Unable to relax his mind Max decides to head home, in the hope to sleep off the emotional overflow.

"Well, well, well, what have we here... Our buddy boys been crying like a baby" spoke a voice from the park Max walked alongside. Glancing through the fence into the park, through the darkness of the night that swallowed everything not touched by the light glow of the dim street lamp blinking aimlessly above him. "James," said Max, who instantly began running as James and his friends charged for him.

"Come here you pussy!" yelled Adam, as James accomplice was hot on Max's tail. Already exhausted from the gym session, Max's bruised and battered body continued to propel itself forward, panting heavily he can hear the footsteps of the trio getting louder and louder as their un-exerted bodies gained on him. A cold hand grabs his shoulder gripping his hoodie tightly and tugging backwards so as to slow the propulsion of Max, who chokes slightly from the sudden restriction of air cut off by his hoodie. Coming to a stop Max spins, pivoting on his toes instinctively as a natural reflex from his rigorous training Max throws his elbow with brutal precision and force. His elbow clashes with Adam's nose, the crunch barely noticeable over the yelp of pain Adam shrieks, as he is sent tumbling into the thorn bush of the garden beside them.

"Arghhh!" bellows James who rugby tackles Max, lifting his puppet like body up before slamming down hard against the unforgiving concrete pavement below. James lay on top of Max throwing a wild flurry of punches in the violent attempt to render him unconscious once again. "Hook the arm, hook the foot, twist your shoulders and hips, then roll!" Jack's words echo in his mind as clear as when they were spoken in training. Max follows these steps reversing the position so he is now on top of James, throwing one individual but satisfying punch stunning James, Max takes off in a sprint while James other friend froze unsure of whether to attempt a one on one with him.

Max runs home, a grin plastered across his face for having beaten his foe, his eyes still burning from the excessive crying before. He opens his front door, running straight upstairs to the bathroom and locking himself inside so as to not be disturbed. Max desperately scrubs at the elbow of his grey hoodie, the blood from Adams nose splattered across it refusing to be fully washed away with soap and water. "Max are you ok love?" his mum called up the stairs clearly startled by his swift entrance. "I'm fine mum, just needed the toilet" Max replied in the hope this awkward answer would prevent any further questions from arising, which thankfully it did.

CHAPTER 2:
UNEXPECTED VISITOR

Reluctantly Max ditches his blood-stained hoodie in a bin on his first day back to work. Dreading the moment with the utmost intensity, the money a seemingly unworthy reward for the mental debilitating torture of standing behind the till serving others with a fake persona so as to portray great customer service and a love for the job as opposed to the poorly disguised truth of unrelenting dread. He arrived at his store, greeted back by his manager, a tall slim woman whose false sense of power was drowned by the abundance of perfume emitting from her, without hesitation she put Max straight on the tills again to continue his torturous existence.

For the next two hours the repetitive drag of repeating the words "Hi, can you come over please" and "would you like a bag?" drove Max to the point of near insanity along with the beep as each product passed over the scanner. His reluctance to work here was not because of laziness however, it was due to the scrutinizing glare his manager gave him and the consistent messages voiced over the speakerphone as Max once again does something considered unfavourably wrong such as lean on the counter. For lack of a better word, she was a bitch, her vengeful glare constantly burning into the back of Max's head as if passing through the CCTV cameras lens as she so eagerly watched him, endlessly waiting for an excuse to raise an issue and once again stamp her unearned authority on her employees and especially the youngest, Max.

The ticking of the large clock mounted on the wall behind the counter which Max worked from was so slow, its large hands seemingly hesitating between ticks as time dragged making the last hour of work feel like an eternity. Max took his toilet break, with enthusiastic joy as he had an idea that might create a more pleasant work environment for the last hour. He pulled out his phone and in ear headphones, plugging in one ear and running the wire underneath his shirt and into his ear, being sure to smooth his hair over the ear to mask this luxury. Max chose his favourite radio station on his phone before leaving the toilet and heading back to the counter which held him like a prison.

"Breaking news heading across the South Coast in the county of Winterbourne, we are being urged to ask all members of the public to remain in their homes as a matter of security!" yelled a panic stricken news reporter from the radio. Max listened eagerly, he could hear the genuine fear projecting through his earpiece. "The government aren't currently presenting any more details but we are in contact with the military and will keep you all informed should more information about this bizarre scenario come to light." Continued the reporter, slowly attempting to revert his composure to its previously confident state. "What a load of rubbish" Max giggled to himself, as the top 40 hits began playing again as if to devoid the mass panic the previous statement of urgency may have induced.

The sound of sirens whirred in the background, their whining echo edging closer and closer, and a slight vibration overhead as a helicopter zoomed past. "Bing" the entrance bell rang as a short, extremely thin man rushed through the door, pushing it forcefully as he gasped for air, frantically searching the environment with his eyes. The short middle-aged man wore round small glasses, perched up on his large nose, his grey hair was scruffy as if having battled with the elements outside and sweat stains marked the armpits of the long lab coat he was wearing.

His head continued to bob around scanning the area until it stopped as he locked eyes with Max, marching with a surprising pace for such a short legged man he lent over the counter staring directly at Max as he did so. "Please, please boy you have to hide me, I have uncovered a dark secret and they aim to extinguish the truth we all deserve." whispered the man whose words were spoken cautiously as if not wanting anyone to hear, even though the shop was deserted. "Please!" the man begged again, his unquestionable fear of something catching him apparent through the nervous twitches with which he gazed out of the window and back to Max's eyes.

"Ok" said Max, his gut feeling overruling his mind's instinctual need to avoid this stranger with extreme prejudice. The stranger's eyes lit up with a glimmer of hope, "behind here under the counter" spoke Max sternly, now anxious as to what to expect walking through his door. The man squeezed under the counter so he was no longer visible to anyone but Max who glanced nervously in his direction. "Ding" went the bell as three military men burst through the door, their mp5 machine guns raised and spreading to scope the shop, "all clear" yelled the larger of the three men after scanning the shop. Stood with his hands raised empty above his head Max shook with fear, his eyes clasped firmly shut as if this dream would miraculously disappear when he chooses to open them.

"Max?" spoke one of the officers staring down at his name badge, with his gun now lowered. Max slowly opened his eyes, anxiously expecting these moments to be his last for harbouring what must be a fugitive. "We are sorry to startle you, have you seen a middle-aged man about five foot five inches wearing a lab coat?" asked the man, his eyes intensely analysing Max's body language for clues as to his honesty. "N-No" answered Max sheepishly, staring at the guns resting on the military vests of the three operatives.

Three more blacked out SUVs squealed to a halt in front of the store, the doors swinging open to reveal more operatives jumping out and raising their guns, the red dot sights reflecting off the storefronts glass, causing Max's heart rate to continue dramatically rising. Max stares in a daydream fashion towards the scene which was unfolding before him, his heart-beat so loud now he can only faintly hear over it, it pounded unendingly feeling as though it may break free from his chest.

"And who are you!" screeched his manager's voice from the back of the store as she barged through the swinging doors to present herself to the unwelcome hostiles in her store. Pivoting instantly whilst raising their guns quickly to aim the aggressor she quickly shuts up and raises her hands. "We are hunting for a violent, psychopathic fugitive who has escaped custody and is in the area, if you see anything suspicious or anyone mildly resembles the afore-mentioned person then ring 999 and we will arrive" grunted the smaller of the three operatives before exiting the store followed by his colleagues.

Max began to smirk as he replayed the glorious moment his manager was held at gunpoint, before snapping back to reality as she slammed her scrawny hand down on the counter. "Don't you ever tell anyone about what just happened or you can kiss your job goodbye!" screamed his manager before skulking back to her cave, the office out back. Max looked down as the man began to crawl out from underneath the counter. "Thank you" he spoke sincerely. "All they say about me is rubbish, all I've wanted my whole life is the ability to help people, that's been my biggest goal and my greatest achievement, for I now have this ability and will give it to you" he finished.

Extending his hand to shake Max's he pulls him close, "Ouch what the hell!" yelped Max taken aback by the stinging sensation in his shoulder. Looking down, he sees an emptied syringe lodged into his shoulders muscle, "What the heck did you inject in..." his words are cut short as he slurs and collapses onto the cold hard floor beneath him. Totally paralysed but still awake Max could all but look up at the stranger, who crouched down staring at the corpse like person crippled before him "You, will have to do". The man wearily rose to his feet before leaving the store and the weakened Max behind.

Ten minutes passed, as Max laid there continuing to stare at the store's ceiling whilst his body felt like it de-thawed from its frozen state. Knowingly trembling, Max's concentration was paying off as his toes began to respond to his commands by twitching. "What's happening to me? Who the hell was that man? What's he injected me with? Am I gonna die?!"

Max's inner monologue ran in a flurry of panic, searching desperately for any logical answer that could piece together a reasonable explanation that may answer any of the questions swarming through his brain. As his body begins to regain its consciousness Max is able to move more and more first rolling onto his front and using his arms and legs to push his body upright until limpidly he stands, swaying in a drunk like manner and still slightly dizzy.

"What on God's green earth have you been doing!" screamed his manager through the store com speakers, "you have been off camera for almost ten minutes!" she continued. Her words were more aggravating than Max had previously acknowledged, his rage beginning to build as she continued to hurl abuse through the speakers at him, each word adding timber to the already burning fire inside him. "Will you just shut up" Max screamed, finally adopting the same rude, unforgiving approach his manager had inflicted upon him for the painstaking eight months of employment. "I quit" he finished, the fire of his rage now extinguished with a satisfying and soothing breeze as he releases the control with which it has over him.

Max walked out of the store, a grin stretched from cheek to cheek, "oh, did I tell her, silly cow" he said, chuckling to himself in amusement as he journeyed back home. The burden of work was no longer looming over him like a stormy cloud instead the sense of pure delight gleaming from inside him so brightly that he almost forgot the events that led to the final decisive moment he quit.

"What on earth?" questioned Max, now back in the safety and comfort of his bedroom. Max's more muscular, toned physique stared back at him as stood topless gazing intensely into the long standing mirror beside his wardrobe. His eyes thoroughly scanned the area around his shoulder, inspecting his injury. The mark where he was injected was slightly raised in a discoloured lump, the veins around it pressing against his near transparent skin with a tinge of green protruding from beneath them. "Are you ok Max, or have you decided we won't be gifted by your presence!" bellowed his mum up the stairs, loud enough to stop his dog from barking and to break Max's concentration as he focused on his wound. "Alright!" yelled Max the annoyance clear within his words. Grabbing his microwave dinner and putting it on a tray, Max headed into the lounge throwing himself into the soft cushions of the sofa before switching on the news and tucking into his dinner.

"The government have just released an image of the assailant, be warned he is armed and dangerous, do not approach him at all costs!" blurted the crackled sound of the reporter's voice. Max looked up, his fork paused in motion half way up to his open mouth, staring at the screen with dread as he recognised the picture of the face to be that of the man who he harboured. "What's up Max?" spoke a soft squeaky voice from the beanbag in the corner of the room, turning his head to see his sister, a short, innocent looking, sweet child who gazed at Max with admiration. "Nothing to worry about sis" Max replied, masking his emotion so as not to worry his little sister Jess. His appetite swiftly left him as the realisation that he had come face to face with the wanted man dwelled on him.

"Professor Krunan, the well renowned physicist is believed to be in possession of a highly dangerous chemical compound, which the government urgently require to obtain safely again" continued the reporter. "If anyone sees or comes into contact with the fugitive please call 999 immediately" finished the reporter before switching to the next story. "Dangerous chemical compound is that what the bastard injected me with?" thought Max, his body beginning to shake as the anxiety of his potential death replayed over and over in his mind.

Leaving his tray on the seat and exiting the room Max rushed upstairs shutting the door to his room as he leapt onto his bed, opening the lid of his laptop. Frantically typing 'Professor Krunan physicist' into the search bar of his browser, thousands of results were instantly loaded and Max sat until late that night researching his work, any biographies, videos, reports, studies of the professor he could find, compiling his results into one folder on his Desktop. His results so far explained that professor Krunan was a physicist who specialised in genetic architecture research, his latest exploits involved the transmutation of genetic architectures but clinical trials had yet to be orchestrated. Max unwillingly closed his eyes as his eyelids heaviness was too great to continue the struggle of keeping them open.

CHAPTER 3: A PLACE
IN THE SHADOWS

"**A**rgh!" Max screamed the next morning waking himself with the abrupt sound he unknowingly projected. His bed was soaked through with sweat but his skin ice cold as he sat up his mind slowly began to kick into action. He took off his top and stood once again in front of the mirror to examine his wound's condition after yesterday's vulgar appearance. "What the bloody heck is going on?" Max said to himself rubbing the now unmarked piece of skin which shows no sign of having ever been harmed as it was yesterday. "Was it a dream? Please say it was a dream" Max said wishfully to himself grabbing his TV's remote and switching on the nine o'clock news. "Thankfully the fugitive, Professor Kunan has been apprehended by the authorities late last night in the lower east downtown mall. In other news..." the female reporter continued Max cutting her line short as he switched off the TV and threw the remote against his wall in aggression, completely shattering it.

After chucking on some clothes and scoffing down his breakfast of untoasted buttered bagels, Max stormed out of the house, still agitated by the anxiety that the incident which occurred wasn't a dream and that his only proof of contact, was the mark on his skin, which no longer there. "Who's going to believe me? And what the bloody heck did he inject me with?" Max thought, his cluelessness further provoking his aggression. He began his least favourite journey of walking to school while pondering these questions endlessly, no answers arising from his consciousness.

"Get him!" yelled a voice coming from closely behind him, instantly recognisable as his arch enemy James. Max took off into a sprint as if chased by an enraged lion, sprinting with every ounce of energy contained within his body, kicking over dustbins as he passed them so as to hopefully slow the predators avidly chasing him. "Catch that little prick!" screamed James desperately fearing the loss of an opportunity he did not want to miss. Max glanced over his shoulder to see a shimmer of light reflecting from James hand, from a knife clasped so tightly his white knuckles bulged through his skin.

"No" Max gasped tripping down the curb and falling helplessly into the road, he glanced back quickly to see a smirk stretch across his adversaries face. A screeching noise rung through Max's head, turning quickly to ascertain the location from which the noise was coming from. A large lorry was gaining on him, smoke rising from the tires as they were locked by the brakes which desperately struggled to stop the vehicle, a chubby faced man in the driver's seat, a pure expression of fear written across his face as he came to the unsurmountable decision that he would not be able to stop in time. Each second passing as though they were minutes as Max witnessed what would be his demise edging uncontrollably closer and closer. Reaching out Max touched the ground the lorries large stature blocking out the sunlight as he feels the stony course tarmac between his fingers for the last time, and everything instantly faded to black.

"Oh my god!" yelled the truck driver, jumping out of his truck desperate to see an alive body instead of a corpse. James, Adam and Mick stop on the edge of the road dazzled at what they just witnessed even they gasped with the anticipation of knowing whether Max is dead, has the truck driver saved James a prison sentence? There is no display of damage to the front of the truck so the driver rushes towards the back, checking all of the wheels and expecting to discover a bloody, tangled corpse warped between them. "What in god's name?" the driver spoke aloud as no remnants of his victim are there. James yells across to the driver "Is Max ok?" not because he is genuinely worried but more out spite and his need for clarification. "It's like he has vanished into thin air!?" replied the driver sheep-

ishly walking around the truck with a look of bewilderment stretched across his fat squashed face.

"W-What just happened? Am I dead? I remember a
truck?" questioned Max, moving both his head and
body but unable to see anything but complete darkness. Max stands up unable to feel the consistency of
anything except the floor beneath his feet. Blinking
rapidly Max hopes to see something, some semblance of light or the outline of an object around him,
but is sadly let down. Hopelessly moving forwards,
Max anxiously began to take step after step, "Where
am I?" he pleads, his voice eerily fading off into the
distance of the clearly vast blank space surrounding
him.

Step by step Max begins to increase his speed trust-
ing that the very ground he can feel beneath his
feet won't disappear like all light has from this vast
ether he has found himself in. "I can do this!" Max
said, as he elevated his speed until he was actively
running, "I will find somewhere, someone, I need to,
I refuse to quit!" he panted as hurls into a fast sprint.
Thirty seconds later, panting heavy Max slows to a
stop, his body begging for just a drop of water to
quench his thirst, he drops to his knees slamming
his hands against the floor in despair, pure hopelessness. "Was my life not enough! What more can
you take from me!" he screamed in rage, admittedly
with the hope that some entity would at least hear
him and offer their assistance.

Max lifted his head slowly turning it in an attempt to see something, anything... "Wait... Is that?" he whispers, squinting unsure whether it is a small light he can see extremely far in the distance. Unsure of whether his mind was in fact playing tricks on him for wanting some guidance so desperately. Rising like an Olympic Sprinter he sped off towards the light, as he got closer and closer the light grew bigger and bigger no distinct outlines behind it but hope rang in Max's mind and he refused to stop until he reached his objective.

"What the hell?" whispered Max, stood dauntingly in front of a huge glowing sphere of light. "What is this?" Max questioned as he circled the large floating object. Slowly and anxiously Max raises his hand hovering millimetres before the object's surface debating whether to touch it. Ripples materialise as his fingertips touch the warm water like consistency that stands before him. "How strange is this? Am I dead? Is this a dream? This can't be real, but... it feels so genuine" Max continued to mentally quiz himself bewildered as he plunges his hand into the water like surface.

"Arghhhhh" screamed Max, as blinding flashes of light pulse from the circular object like flashbangs in his face, the previously silent environment was now crackling and sizzling as light leapt fluidly from the surface, small glowing spheres arise arising slowly from the surface as if being born, before propelling themselves rapidly into the furthest corners of the darkness. Removing his hand from the light quickly Max tripped backwards onto the floor, staring helplessly as the circle began shrinking as more and more light left it. Bang, the light had all but disappeared before exploding, its noise ringing through his head as he clutches his ears and closes his eyes as the largest outburst of light yet blinded him, feeling as though it had burnt even the retinas that sit behind his eyes.

The blurriness of Max's eyes cleared slowly, white specks floating around his vision. His eyesight cleared and Max rose slowly to his feet, excitement and curiosity releasing a surge of adrenaline into his bloodstream as his eyes eagerly scanned his environment. The environment was no longer shrouded by an empty darkness, instead was a dimly lit and colourless as if stepping directly into a black and white film. The previously released glows of white essence were still visible; each crammed into what should have been the darkest crevices of the environment surrounding him.

"At least we don't have to worry about that stupid dweeb anymore" sniggered a voice Max recognised all too well. Spinning one hundred and eighty degrees on the spot, Max's perception was correct, his eyes locked clearly on James and his two groupie accomplices. After a few seconds, Max realised this wasn't an empty hope draining abyss; this was just another perspective of what was his actual world. The truck which should have ended his existence undeniably towered above him, its wide eyed frantic driver still pacing around panicking about the seemingly unavoidable accident he was just a part of.

Max stared down at the glowing pulsating floor where he had previously vanished into this secondary world. A mirage hovered above the floor's light as it emitted a heat like energy, drawing Max's curiosity closer and closer until he felt the compulsive need to jump into the glow as if a child leaping to stomp down into a puddle as a child. "What the hell!" yelped James an irrational fear present in his voice as he froze in place momentarily before taking off in a sprint, closely followed by his two gob-smacked sidekicks.

Max stood in place, glancing down at his now colourful hands again, the rest of his body continuing to rise from the truck's shadow, which had previously swallowed him. He continued materialising back to reality as if rising from the sea to the shoreline until he stood firm footed back in reality, "w-what just happened to me?" Max questioned both fearful and mildly excited at the unique experience he had just encountered. Two hands firmly grabbed each arm spinning and shaking him simultaneously, Max's eyes locked with the small truck driver who had emerged from the back of the truck after completing his inspection. The small sweaty man considerately mumbled "Thank god, thank god, it's a miracle, praise god" with a wide outstretched smile stretched from cheek to cheek. "Are you ok kid?" he questioned, anticipation echoing in his voice as the reality that his victim wasn't in fact a mentally conceived image placed to taunt the integrity of his mind. "Yes I'm fine" hastily replied Max, who took off in a quick walk, eager to continue his contemplation of what had just happened to him.

The rest of the day flashed past with extreme speed, Max's mind frantically recollecting his memories of the experience, struggling to unravel how the experience came to pass. Were it not for the occasional taunts of "freak" from James and his accomplices, throughout the day then Max would not believe it had actually happened. The day continued to drift past whilst no further clues presented themselves to Max about the incident, hoping to get a good night's sleep and come to a definitive conclusion of the events by morning Max allowed his mind to wander and floated off into a deep sleep.

CHAPTER 4: THE TRANSITION

"**M**axxxx!" screamed his mother endlessly in the same tired, but aggressively authoritative voice, startling Max from his deep sleep. "Ok mum" Max sighed, the foggy haze of tiredness still blurring his vision as he sits upright and lifts his head to face the tall ornately carved frame of his mirror. "Oh my... What on earth?" Max questioned, rising to his feet and striding towards the mirror. His reflection stared back at him, there his body stood rigid, his abdomen now defined, his arms larger and muscular, and his physique generally thicker and more muscular. "I'm leaving" his mum once again interrupting Max whilst in his pondering state, who rushed downstairs ready for the lift to school, she had promised.

Max's arrival to school somewhat resembled a celebrity arriving at a red carpet event, he left the vehicle saying "bye" to his mother and then was greeted by the eyes of every student in the parking lot. They were all staring and sniggering, Max realised finally after an initial feeling of sunken awkwardness, that James must have been spreading the rumours around the school like a giant game of Chinese whispers. People parted to allow Max through as he headed into the crowd aiming for the schools entrance, Max could hear but chose to ignore the few words he could hear through the mumbles, such as; witch, freak, mutant, weirdo.

The scolding eyes of James burnt into the back of Max's head during class, his glare constant and relentless as Max sat helplessly at the front of the class, since his outbreak of rage the other day. Max felt slightly anxious sitting in his new position as his back was facing towards his enemy and although he knew the teacher was present he couldn't help but feel apprehensive, as if expecting an impending attack from James. The bell rang, causing Max's scrunched up shoulders to relax with the knowledge he no longer had to worry about being blindsided in his current vulnerable seating position, a predicament placed on him by Mr Baldwick, his antagonistic teacher.

The day before still resounded through Max's mind like a daydream, and if it weren't for the consistent reminders by his classmates through their sniping comments, Max would put it down as an elusive incident manifested within his imagination. "How did I do it? Was it a one off? Could it happen again? What do I remember?" Max questioned himself thoroughly in such a way even a professional inter-rogator could have appreciated. He sat alone on a table in the cafeteria, out casted as if some kind of leper. "I remember James, Adam and Nick chasing me, James had a knife and I tripped into the road..." Max recollected, a frowning squint of concentra-tion pressed across his face, as he climbed back in his memory.

Squelch, a moist warm sensation spreads across Max's back as he is nudged forward in his seat with force. "Sorry mate" spoke a voice as Max quickly turned his head to face the assailant, the smug look of joy evident from his teeth bearing grin, whose now empty plate was clutched in his hand as his lunch continued to roll down Max's back. The stu-dents filling the cafeteria howled with laughter, pointing and sniggering once again at Max's expense whose body began to pulse with adrenaline, shak-ing intensely with pure ferocious un-negotiable rage, "James!" Max screamed, rising from his chair to uppercut the jaw of the larger foe James.

Expecting a rise from the emotionally unstable Max, James parried the evident uppercut of Max whose fist glided unsuccessfully past his target. Crunch, an unexpected force exploded into Max's side lifting him from the floor and crashing him down into the barrage of chairs that sat beside him innocently on his unoccupied table. Adam had clearly decided to join in with the fight by tackling the unaware Max's blindside. A circle is formed by a crowd of students who rushed to surround the trio, the flashes of their phones drowning Max's vision like a group of paparazzi scrambling for the perfect shot, as they avidly enjoy the spectacle before them. Bench pressing the dead weight of Adam from his body Max rolled free of the unconscious scoundrel whose head had collided with the table on the downward journey of his tackle.

Max rose quickly to his feet swiftly raising his knee in a fluid but forceful motion crashing into James's groin, like a powerful wave crashing against the breakers of the beach, instantly immobilising James who curled over in agonising pain panting like a dog thirsting for water. Max charged at the crowd to break free of the circle that formed the equivalent of a human cage around him, sending the front viewers tumbling backwards into the crowd squashed in behind them, simulating a domino effect as they began to topple.

Max paced through the hallway that led to his previous fight club styled arena, breathing heavily as attempted to console his vengeful enraged self. "I can't do this anymore!" he yelled aggressively, punching wildly into the lockers that lined the corridor as he passed by them, eventually throwing a punch against the wall. "Holy s...." Max paused, his hand and forearm no longer visible as enshrouded by the blackness of the shadow formed against the wall by the light bouncing off the lockers beside it, a warm liquid sensation present on his fingertips.

"That's it!" Max bellowed excitedly as his mind was flooded with the memories he had so desperately searched for, the truck, the shadow, him sinking into this parallel universe. Unconfidently, Max stepped forwards crouching to get his head through into the shade as he is once again greeted by the black and white surroundings of the shadow world, resembling the school he had just left with impeccable indifference, the wall where Max's shadow gateway into this realm stood glowed with a blindingly bright white light. Curiously Max pressed his head through the white shimmering surface and was greeted once again with the colour and warmth of the real world as his senses adjusted to the contrasting difference, before drawing it back into the colder darker realm the rest of his body stood within.

Max retraced his footsteps down the corridor he had just hastily left moments before, walking into the full cafeteria, he could hear the students gossiping about the events that had occurred, and Mr Phillips now stood tall statured above James and Adam who sheepishly in the face of authority apologised but were whisked away to his office via the corridor on the opposite side of the cafeteria, parallel to the one where Max stood. Shouting "unlucky" Max expected heads to turn, but no-one responded or even turned to see who had shouted, almost like his voice was unheard to those around him.

Max walked towards Mr Baldwick who stood in the

hallway to ensure no further trouble ensued, "Sir, I'm sorry they started it" he sincerely spoke, but Mr Baldwick looked directly through Max as if unaware of his presence. "Sir?" asked Max again, trying to grasp his attention but to no avail, "Rowan sit down and eat or that's one hour detention for you!" Mr Baldwick yelled, raising his hand to point at the victim of his deathly gaze. Max stared down in astonishment as Mr Baldwick's hand protruded into his chest with his pointing gesture, but Max felt absolutely nothing. "They can't hear, see or feel me, I'm free" Max whispered grinning avidly with excitement at his new found freedom from being gawked at as the awkward, loner, weirdo people portrayed him as.

Max left the school grounds; walking into the main high street of town which was crammed with people, he walked calmly through them taking in the evident shadows through which he could reveal himself. Looking up to the sky, Max couldn't help but notice the glimmer of what looked like giant spider webs splayed across the rooftops, between lampposts and in the crevices of the building structures around him. "What in god's name?" Max inquisitively whispered, knowing that these are not apparent to the members of the public walking blissfully along in the real world.

Beginning to run he headed for Creacher Woods, the place locals rumoured to be haunted. From a young age all parents urged their children to steer clear of creacher woods, mainly due to addict users residing within the treelines, ready to rob any innocent person who enters the vale of darkness, sitting beneath the canopy of tall trees overhead. But many rumours hinting to a past in witchcraft, and legends, spread from across the hundred thousand acre woodland. Being the only local spot with a mythical background Max can't resist the hope that he may be able to find more answers about what's happened to him or even better find others like himself.

Max becomes more and more relaxed as he runs and unknowingly his speed continued to increase, his feet moving faster and faster effortlessly, becoming blurs beneath him, the wind slapping his face harshly as his hair sweeps back fully revealing Max's face, the world around him channels into a blurred clarity of tunnel vision as Max runs alongside the cars on a thirty mile an hour road with ease. "Woo hoooo" screamed Max with joy overwhelmed by the sensations his body was feeling, as he quickly descended on the treeline of Creacher woods whose interior glowed with a strong white due to the many shadows created by the treeline. "Here goes nothing" he thinks slowing down rapidly before entering the woods due to the fear of tripping on one of the many roots protruding from the ground beneath him.

A deadly silence filled the air, the atmosphere dropping to a darkened state of lifeless emptiness. His dark surroundings shrouded in the thick, sticky webs bridged between the branches overhead, and the ground cracked, dry and unforgivingly dark, the shadows light being the only thing keeping Max from being within an endless ether of darkness as when he first entered the shadow realm. The trees stood tall above him, he imagined in the real world he would see their thick green canopy, but instead here they act only as a hindrance; Blocking out what little light the sun could provide as it pushes through the leaves allowing only the gentlest touch of sunlight on the open patches of ground visible through the open patches of the canopy.

Max continued his escapade further into the woods, swallowing loudly as the anticipation of meeting others like himself grew alongside the scapegoated fear the forest evoked. As he delved deeper into the forest squeezing between the thick dark bushes contaminating almost everywhere but a small trail worming between the roots. This small trail guiding him to the point where the road behind him was no longer visible through the layers of shrubbery he was contained within. "Well this place is as freaky as they say" Max giggled, continuing nervously on.

"Ouch" he yelped as he tripped in the slightest of holes in the track, bringing his body harshly down to its knees. "I've been walking for forty minutes and everything just looks exactly the same!" he grunted out of aggravated annoyance. Cupping his hands around his mouth in a ludacris frenzy of impatience Max yelled "Helloooo!" hoping for that his quest would be successful if only someone replied to the hopeful call.

The sound of scuttling filled the air like a thousand quick footsteps were charging down upon him. Max froze, the noise unsettling him instantly as although hopeful for a response from the desperate plea he bellowed, the extravagance of the noise echoing through the forest, sounded as though an army descended on his position, giving Max the doubtable feeling that whatever was coming would not be an ally.

A small opening was evident not too far ahead, Max charged for it as though an open space may help remove the now disconcerting claustrophobia he now encountered whilst understanding how lost and alone he truly is. The noise got evidently louder and louder, its echo ringing in Max's ear like a whisper from death itself. "I should have been patient, shit, what should I do?" Max muttered with an urgency as his eyes scoured the shrubbery surrounding him, hoping for the light of a shadow to capture his eyes so that he could escape whatever he had awoken. The clattering was almost upon him, twenty metres, ten metres, 5 metres, Max's heart pounding, his hands clammy as adrenaline is released into his bloodstream, causing his muscles to twitch and shake in the apprehension of danger that loomed before him. Silence... The clattering eerily stopped, Max breathed a heavy sigh, feeling surely surrounded and viewed upon like a victim being unconsciously skulked upon by a stalker. Skinting slightly whilst clenching his hands into fists Max lent forward as he spotted a smaller shimmer of light within the bush directly in front of him.

"What on earth is that?" Max pondered nervously, "arghhhhh!" he screamed tripping backwards as the creature pounced from its vantage point through the bush, its legs ripping through the intertwined stems that kept the wild plant together, two pincers opened and ready to bite down upon its prey unforgivingly as its screech rung through his ears, partially deafening the overwhelmed carcass of the downed teenager. "What the fuck!" Max screamed, scrambling backwards frantically across the floor on which he now lay helpless, staring up at his aggressor. It's eight eyes stared hungrily back at him, its spike tipped eight legs extending to allow the now roughly seven foot spider to tower over Max, its bulbous back curled, a sharp spear like stinger protruding from its end, as its pincers snap repeatedly on its approach so as to further taunt the devastated teenager before it.

"Go!" Max's instincts yelled at him, somewhat awakening him from his current frozen state, as he lay before what he could only ever have imagined to be real. His feet scrambled on the floor for traction, as the creature lunged down upon him ready to deliver its killing blow, Max's foot finally successfully delivering the traction necessary as he pushed up and turned narrowly missing the two pincers which crunched through the floor where he had been but a moment before. Max ran like an all-star athlete re-tracing his steps through down the overgrown track which had almost led him to his demise.

His aggressor pursues quickly, its legs stamping against the ground which such speed it already began to gain on its target. "Oh noooo!" Max howled, sliding hastily along the floor so as to narrowly avoid another spider which leapt from the bush beside him, further slowing his escape. His reactions, clearly much sharper than ever before; as he managed to foresee the event in an almost slow motion transition as soon as the bush began to part from the creatures large stature bounding through it. What Max could only assume was the alpha spider, due to its first solo attack, was now only three metres behind him as he glanced quickly across his shoulder, the bushes behind him all rust-ling making Max aware of the pack now hunting him.

"Shadow, Shadow, shadow... come on!!" Max panted, as he bounded down the track, marginally avoiding any stray roots along the track and grasp-ing the low hanging branches of trees so as to propel his body quicker around the sharp turns as he navi-gated down the route with speed and precision. His eyes frantically scan his now blurred surroundings where his swiftness granted only a channelled field of vision, searching for that escape, the spot that will grant his freedom back to reality.

Snap, snap, snap! The noise crunches away behind getting closer and closer is it snaps at his heels. Every single movement now a fluid attempt to dodge the alpha's attacks whilst maintaining his escape. "There!" A glimmer of light catches Max's eyes like a gift from the gods, it stemmed from a burrow beneath a tree in amongst its hollowed trunk only 30 metres ahead. "You can make it" Max reassured himself wishfully as the tree drew closer and closer now only five metres ahead. "Arghh" Max yelps sliding into the light of the shadow and back into the real world, the spider's unsuccessful attack managed to cut along his back as he transitioned into his slide, the one pincer hooking his skin and ripping through it with ease.

Max lay there staring up at the now green canopy above him, the glimmers of light shining like diamonds as the wind gently blows the leaves creating a glittery ceiling to the dark forest. A warm sharp pain burned in Max's back as he rolled onto his front clutching at his back and feeling a warm moisture through his ragged t-shirt. Looking down at his hand he sees red, a lot of blood covering his hand, "What happens in the shadow realm carries across into the real world?" he muttered still staring down at the blood spread across his palm and fingertips. "Fine, you want real!" he grunted, rising to his feet, his fear of the spiders and the pain he felt creating a heroic confidence, a dominant pride of disallowing anyone or anything to control his emotions except himself.

Max begins to climb the tree from whose hollow trunk he had emerged quickly thrusting himself up powered by the feeling inside him. Stopping by another hollow in the trees surface about five metres from the ground, grasping the thick branch overhead he swung his body into the hollow emerging once again in the shadow world but this time five metres above the spider which still stood by the hollow beneath him. "Arrrrrgh!!" Max bellowed like a lion roaring with the dominant confidence of his supremacy over his enemy, his body scrunched up as he fell actively through the air down upon his pursuer. Looking at his fingertips enticingly they manifest into shadowlike claws razor sharp and capable of tearing through anything with the fluidity of a knife through butter.

He lands on the neck of the spider, as if preparing to ride the beast which so passionately hunted him, it's cold shell like skin doing nothing to cushion his landing as the pointed tips of its feet dig further into the ground beneath them due to the added weight Max's body provided. In a swift thrusting motion Max plunges down his claw, its sharp tips penetrating the shell like top of the spider's head, black liquid seeping uncontrollably through the openings his hand made. "You will never hurt anyone again!" Max spoke, his words loud and clear as he grasped the brain like ball within the head, squeezing and ripping it free of its protective shell, each muscle releasing its hold due to the force with which his hand retracted until he held it proudly above his head, the spiders corpse collapsing beneath him as all motor functionality stops, and its legs are no longer prepared to hold the weight of the dead carcass above them. Dismounting from the spider's neck Max turns towards his other pursuers, the accomplices who also hunted him, all but two of them retreated hastily back into the deep darkened woods behind them, after witnessing their alphas decapitation. Max looked admiringly towards his hand, finally acknowledging the majestic beauty of the blades manifested on his fingertips forming a claw-like surface similar to the werewolves he had seen whilst secretly watching his mother's old horror movies. Squeezing tightly on the brain in his hand until it pops Max yells "Well come on" at the two remaining adversaries who dare challenge his now prominent sense of pride and justice.

The larger of the two spiders leaps first its pincers snapping with devastating force that would crush through steel. Max's instinct came into play yet again, his senses becoming more attuned to the visceral predator his body was capable of becoming, lunging forwards he grabs the front of the two pincers aiming to tear him apart, the force and strength of the spiders attack sliding his feet back through the rough floor beneath them, pushing him backwards about three metres into the side of the hollowed trunk just next to its opening. Fighting with every muscle in his body Max held the pincers which inch by inch pressed closer to his face, each swipe of them closely fanning Max's panic stricken face as he began to doubt his previous realisation of his strength.

In that moment as Max's demise became a truly imminent possibility his mind wandered, flashing through the series of events that had led to him being in this scenario; The vulnerability he had felt when bullied, the strength he felt when he stood up to them, the scientist, the truck, everything streaming together into a fluid photolike montage of the past few months of his life. The pincers now only a cm from the surface of his face, every muscle in his body shaking as he struggles to resist the power being pressed upon him, refusing to give in willingly and allow his attacker the vengeance it so avidly hungered for. "I-I am... not... ready to... die!" he strains, releasing all fear about the future, worries from his past and instead feeling the warm sensation as the force of the darkness around him closes in like a quickly descending mist, its power rising in through his feet, rejuvenating every fibre of his body and granting a strength he had never felt. "Arghhh!" he pushed, now battling the pincers back as if straining to bench press as extremely heavy weight until his arms were outstretched.

Screaming as he strains to do so, Max grips each pincer, pulling each in an opposite direction, widening the pincers reach until he could feel the cracking as they begin to separate from their now retreating scuttling source. Snap! The noise resembling that of a large stick cracking under extreme force, as Max manages to pry free the right pincer, plunging its spike into one of its aggressors eight eyes with such swiftness and brutality it instantly renders the beast deceased.

Lifting his head slightly to view the remaining assailant which turned its back on him, Max smugly smiled, "You give in to ey?" Lifting its tail, a barrage of white wire like substance shoots towards Max's legs, only one of which was able to manoeuvre safely dodging the oncoming attack. Tugging harshly so as to release his left leg from the binding Max was unable to release himself, it's sticky malleable wire consistency had entangled Max binding him to the floor beneath him. "Shit, shit" Max mumbled, grasping his leg with his hands hoping to pull it free of its binding but unfortunately being unsuccessful, the spider ahead of him turns to face its trapped victim, opening its pincers it screeched loudly, alarming Max even more, causing him to panic the same childlike way he had the first time he encountered James. The ground beneath Max's feet began to vibrate as the now familiar sound of scuttling descended on him ready to feast on the murderer of two of their own. "Come on, Max, you gotta do this" he begged frantically scratching at the web with his claws hoping to loosen them enough to just release his leg.

Raising his head he saw the distant bushes shuddering as the flock of spiders drew closer, the ground's vibrations now majorly unsettling Max as they caused his legs to shudder. His entrapper remained in its distant position, staring at the helpless bait with which Max had now become. The bushes surrounding his position flattened as though plowed down by a combine harvester, as what looked like hundreds of spiders charged on his position covering as far as his eye could see. The constant wrenching of his leg finally released him from his bindings and diving for the light in the trees hollow Max hopes and prays to make it in time and not be decapitated by the spiders leaping for him like a dog jumping for a Frisbee.

CHAPTER 5: WHO AM I?

"**M**r Baxter, we are all done now" spoke the soft melodic voice of an elderly nurse, her voice as soothing as the local anaesthetic used to numb the area on his back where he had been cut open. Her surgically gloved hands clutched a hooked needle, used to stitch together the two parts of skin that had been separated by the first spiders' malicious attack. Claiming a trip in the woods and the catch of a sharp branch as the culprit of his medical state, Max had headed to Accident and Emergency after just managing to escape his death. "Max are you ok?" eagerly questioned his mum, the anxious tremor in her voice very much doubting the authenticity of Max's story. "Yes mum, I'll be fine" he spoke responsively, his hands clasped tightly together in his lap, "lets just go home" he pleaded, the tiredness of the day's events having clearly drained the inexperienced Max.

The next few days passed quickly as his overprotective mother nurtured him back to health, taking time off work so as to consistently feed and hydrate Max whose painful condition was only made worse by the frequent disturbances as he tried to sleep. Max's mind slipped and slided between conscious and subconscious thoughts, reliving the events that occurred and piecing together the very informative lessons he had learnt. "So if I'm hurt in there, it carries across back to my real body. There are giant vicious spiders that attack you... avoid their webs. I can manifest claws! I am a lot stronger and faster in that realm I just need to believe in myself" Max spoke as he wrote a list of the lessons he had been taught, so as to not forget or make the same mistakes again, should he be brave enough to venture back into the realm that now has had multiple occasions of near death for him, but the excitement and curiosity coursing through his veins made it almost impossible to consider never venturing back to the place that made him feel so alive.

Unable to participate in the day's physical education lesson which consisted of a warm-up followed by dodgeball, Max sat on the side-lines, a small bench pressed against the back wall of the gymnasium. As enthusiastic as he would have been to participate in one of his favourite lessons, he couldn't help but feel a begrudging annoyance for being forced into submission from the class as his wounds were still healing. Instead using this time to ponder over the potential of his gifts and dwelling on both the good and bad things he could achieve by using these powers.

"Catch!" snarled the familiar spite driven voice of James propelling a dodgeball directly at Max, his intuitive reactions pushing him up from his seated position to catch the ball just before contact with his face, twisting his body back and raising his arm Max prepared a counter throw which launched with indisputable accuracy and overwhelming power causing it to whistle the same way in which a stick swiped through the air does. Crack, the should be relatively soft rubber inflated ball met its target, James head whipping back as though punched by Mike Tyson, one of his front teeth leaving his mouth as the force ripped its root from his gum allowing for a small spurt of blood to leave it gap as James body fell unconscious to the ground.

"Bloody hell!" Mr Baldwick gasped, his swear words not even being acknowledged by the teenagers of the class who starred in bewilderment at James, the hardest boy in school being mutilated by a dodgeball. Their gaze slowly rising from the floored bully now victim to his destroyer, with the same incomprehension that viewers would have had seeing David beat Goliath with all but a stone. "Headmasters office now!" screamed Mr Baldwick now pushing the dead weight of James body into the recovery position, having hoped for an easy lesson whilst standing in for Mr Thompson who was on holiday, and furious for the reaction resembling that from his Maths class earlier in the month.

Max stridded out of the gym slamming the door in frustration as once again his counter attack resulted in only himself being slammed as the instigator, which all his classmates knew was not the case but chose not to inform the teacher so as to protect themselves from future bullying by the infamous James. "Forget this school, forget these knobheads!" Max grunted as he paced quickly down through the cafeteria and down the hallway choosing instead to exit the school rather than be patronised or penalised by his headmaster through no fault of his own actions. "I only need school to get a job and earn money!" he snorted, the rage of unjustified condemnation still lingering inside him, "If I want money then I'll just take it" he snarled, as darkened thoughts of money making schemes flooded his mind fuelled by his rage causing an uncharacteristic evil persona to freely toy with the innocence of Max's emotional state of disrepute. "A bank" he queried, his mouth sliding up into a distinct malicious smirk as he headed for town, so as to prove to himself the waste of time school is.

Max approached the bank, his palms sweaty with anxiety as he pondered the way in which he could best get the money from the vault locked within its depths. The large bank sign glowing in the distance only further enticing him to accomplish this feat with a relentless conviction. "You think I need you, I don't need anyone!" he mumbled, his anger still bubbling as though a full kettle was boiling over, his eyeline fixated on the doorway, whilst his mind was planning with inconsequential greed, not truly thinking of the best way in which to approach this undertaking.

"Get down on the bloody ground now! And nobody gets hurt!" roared a voice from within his target, the silhouette of a weapon wielding man distinctly outlined through the translucent entrance doors to the bank which Max finally stood in front of. "Someone's beat me to it!" Max thought, his mind still so tempered he turned his back to leave the scene. The screams of a mother wanting for her baby echoed through the air, the muffled plea ended by a slapping noise as she was struck to the ground after rising to defend her baby which they pried free from its stroller as the ultimate hostage to ensure the reliability of the people's compliance with their orders. "What is the code for the door or I'll blow this baby's head off" bellowed the voice from within, with a ferocity that validated his threats would be fulfilled, his voice only just noticeable over the shrieks of his captives at the prospect of witnessing the deed.

Max hesitated, turning back to face the bank, his rage dropping to a simmer causing for the first time in the last half an hour, a clarity of his pure hearted kindness, which was previously lost to his ego's fury. Max's body yearned to help them, his empathy outweighing the fear of the potential hazards of embarking on a solo rescue as only a teenager. "This is who I am, I am good inside, I can help others, I can make a difference" his affirmations ringing intently inside enthusing him with the positive power necessary to tackle the task at hand with irrefutable wholeheartedness.

Charging at the wall beside the translucent doorway which the silhouetted features were situated behind, Max sunk into the walls shadow, entering the bank in his shadow form he witnessed and quickly assessed the situation surrounding his still healing body. Twelve hostages not including the three bank staff behind there glass protected counter, four robbers, the one closest to the glass counter clutching the baby as he had her in one hand and a sawn off shotgun in the other, of his three accomplices two were armed with machetes and the other with a large military combat knife all brandished to scare the hostages they surrounded in the opposite side of the banks floor. The light from multiple shadows dotted across the bank glistened in Max's eyes as gateways through which he could exact justice and save those as vulnerable as he had been against James in their first encounter.

"Three, two... o..." the baby clutching robber threatened, raising the barrel inline with the child head in his hands, his final count stopped as Max appears from the shadow beside him with an uppercut that startled the larger man, loosening his clutch on the baby he held as Max grabbed and turned quickly sliding the child along the counter and just through the small gap in the glass behind which the cashier sat grabbing the baby to ensure its safety. "You little prick!" bellowed the man raising the shotgun in his hand towards Max who sunk instantly into the shadow on the floor from which he had risen only seconds ago. The large sweaty man glanced around frantically for Max, his eyes darting to every crevice of the room, unsure of what actually just happened, his breath drawing deeply through the thick exterior of the balaclava he wore, his belly protruding in a stained white wife beater worn beneath the green bomber jacket he wore. "Did you see that?" he frantically queried the other three assailants who stood puzzled at the impossible manifestation that had occurred seconds before.

"Arghh" Max screamed leaping ferociously from the shadow beside the shotgun wielding assailant, whose reactions were too slow in twisting to shoot Max, who grabbed the back of his arm, discharging a shotgun shell like a barrage into the wall from which Max had attacked. Max quickly wrestled his larger enemy forcing him to release the shotgun he clutched to so desperately, his other hand reaching into his pocket to reveal a large blade which he quickly slashed and stabbed towards Max, who just managed to dodge each attack. "Ouch" yelled Max as the larger man's foot smashed the air from his chest as he had quickly attacked with the nimbleness of a much smaller man, forcing Max's body to tumble back into the wooden outlined counter.

"You have pissed me off!" screamed the man diving at the dazed Max with the knife outreached , Max grabbed his arm just before the knife plunged into his neck.

"Time to die kid" grunted the larger man, his aggression only overridden by the sweaty stench that intoxicated Max's nose, both people struggling meticulously to win this battle of strength, Max's body shaking as every fibre of his muscle forced itself into action so as to protect against his impending death. "Now" Max thought, leaning quickly to the side and releasing his grip on the knife wielding hand allowing the knife to plunge into the thick wood backdrop where his head was situated a second before. Grasping the back of the balaclava and some of the hair beneath it with his left hand Max repeatedly struck the man's face hastily causing a series of crunching noises as the bones of his face shattered as though brittle sticks were being stomped on. By the fifth punch the fat body of the man weighed down in its entirety on Max as he rolled the unconscious enemy off to his left.

The three remaining assailants stood frozen in the surprise of this mutant like teenager who had just devastated their gun wielding leader. "Kill him" the taller middleman of the three remaining screamed as Max gasped tiredly whilst rising to his feet. His mind raced intuitively scanning the environment hoping to use it as a tool to extinguish the evil twisted bastards before him. Diving back at the wall Max was plunged into the darkness he had now grown customly comfortable with, rolling forwards to enter the light across the other side of the room he revealed himself just beside one of the two machete wielding enemies, grabbing his wielding arm and locking it tightly between max's two arms which tensed quickly causing a snap as his elbow gave way and his arm was rendered useless, the scream of agony tantalisingly punishing Max's eardrum whilst simultaneously acting as a warcry to terrify the remaining two. Twisting his hips as learnt during his mixed martial arts Max threw the thief over his hips hurtling his agonised victim into the ground immobilising him completely.

"Two left" Max thought leaping back into the shadow he had manifested from, only just avoiding the slashing attack of the other machete wielding burglar. Leaping onto the leaflet stand beside him and upwards at the small patch of light formed by a shadow behind the long well-lit lamps in the banks ceiling Max emerged from the ceiling dropping into a seated position on the taller man's shoulders gripping his head tightly between his thighs Max rolled backwards quickly, his force swinging the lanky man like a rag doll over and into the floor where Max sat upright on his neck and delivered the finishing blow to the back of his head to render him out cold. Looking up quickly to see the glint of the combat knives blade swinging swiftly towards him Max rolled to the side avoiding it so narrowly that a small fraction of his hair was sliced off in the process of attempting to dodge the swing. Grabbing the walking stick of the old man laid on the floor submissive to the robbers Max swings it promptly into the temple of his attacker, the thick wooden stump colliding with such force splinters are left in his head as he tumbles incoherently to the floor.

"Police get down!" yelled a large fully armoured man as he and his armed team entered the bank, "You don't move" screamed the officer at Max, the only remaining standing person. Raising his hands above his head Max stepped backwards over the immobilised body of his third victim and sunk into the shadow behind him. "What on god's earth" spoke the officer who stared blankly at the wall, his team cuffing the assailants efficiently. "That boy, he saved my baby, thank you so much child, if you can hear me, thank you" cried the mother as she was assisted to her feet, her face already bruising where she had been struck before Max arrived. Max watched gratefully as the hostages were escorted one by one from the bank, and the mother was reunited with her baby, "Who was the lad who helped you?" questioned the officer still puzzled by Maxs mystical disappearance. "He was an angel in the shadows..." softly spoke the woman, "he was a shadowman".

CHAPTER 6: HUNTED

Max lay daydreaming that night afternoon in the lounge, his mother queried why he was home early and he responsively played the I felt sick card which agonisingly taunted him as his body screamed for the delicious snacks in the cupboard which he couldn't eat without ruining his cover. "I actually did good today, that woman, I like that name; Shadowman, makes me sound like a hero, I mean I suppose I have powers like comic book heroes, I am the good guy after all." Max thought, a good feeling coursing through his veins as he happily has his well-deserved rest.

The front door knocked loudly, slightly startling Max who was fully immersed in his thoughts. "Just coming" innocently shouted his mum, rushing down the stairs towards the door. Her tone changed hastily to an innocent worry, "How can I help you officer?" she asked, Max sat-up quickly on the sofa, "no way can they know it was me at the bank, I-I mean I didn't do anything wrong I just helped them hostages out" Max thought in a mad panic clutching for a possible explanation for his actions. "My name is officer Brunell and this is my colleague officer Nickson, is Max Baxter home?" questioned the officer, his stature imposing his sense of authority over Max's mother, "Y-yes he's just in there" she replied stepping aside and pointing to the door of the lounge.

The officers entered the lounge much to Max's dissatisfaction the taller of the two was a quieter slimmer built man, whilst his partner whose voice Max distinctly noticed from the door was a shorter chubbier man, with a red complexion similar to an overexerted sweaty unfit person. "I'm afraid we are going to have to take a statement from your son Mrs Baxter" spoke the quieter officer, his sincerity emphasising with the worried woman, before her now fearing what her son had been involved in.

Max had a knack of disappearing into the shadows and wished the sofa would just swallow him into the shadow realm so that he may escape this scenario. "What's happened officers?" questioned Max's mother, now standing between the two officers and her stunned son on the sofa. "Your boy was involved in an incident..." spoke one officer, Max's head dropped as he knew they had figured out the teenager from the bank was him, how could he explain what happened to his mother, to anyone without sounding like a crazy person who needs to be locked away. "He has seriously harmed a pupil at school who is now receiving medical care at the hospital, you may have heard of him, James" the second officer continued finishing his quieter halves sentence.

Although he should have been filled with dread Max couldn't help but feel a flurry of relief lifting his spirits, at least the James incident he could explain away. "Well Max...?" questioned his mother a look of disappointment etched into the wrinkled features of her face. "Erm... Well basically I've just gone back to school today and wasn't allowed to do P.E because of the stitches healing from the cut on my back..." Max spoke sheepishly so as to gain the trust of the officers and hopefully help them to be merciful to him. He continued "They were playing dodgeball today, and I was sat on the bench watching, James threw a ball at me, which I caught and threw back I just didn't realise how hard I could throw" Max paused looking up to see his audiences faces, did he need to give a deeper explanation, he wondered.

"You must have one hell of a throw because he has lost a tooth, got a fractured jaw and concussion" spoke the chubby officer, looking un-certainly at Max. "But then instead of going to the headmaster you fled the school grounds" said the taller policeman. Max lowered his head as his mother's gaze lay upon him, daggers of disappointment and distrust at his lack of honesty and lying about being ill. "We are going to have to escort you back to school, and keep this record with us should any insurance claims be made against the school for the allowance of a sport which can actuate such dangerous injuries to be played on its grounds. "Go on Max... Get up and go!" his mum agitatedly hissed at him. As he walked past her escorted by the officers, she continued "We will talk about this when you get home".

Max spent the rest of the day at school in a day-dream, Mr Baldwick allowed him to not visit the headmaster as he could notably see that Max was very reserved upon entering class with the officers. The look on his mother's face scolded into his memory and a feeling of guilt filled him for lying, he knew he had been wrong to lie, but in all sincerity had forgotten about the James incident after being focused on what happened at the bank later that day. Max returned home incident free as his fellow pupils gave him a wide berth at fear he may attack them with his freakish abilities. That night he spoke to his mother, reconciling their differences, and although he didn't state what happened at the bank he made it very apparent that other things were playing on his mind and he feared how she would react should he have said he walked out of school. Max knew clearly he would have to lie again to his mother but came to the realisation that although she doesn't need to know everything if he keeps her involved in big occurrences at school or outside of it then she may be more understanding than he expected.

"Corporal Hopper, you are going to want to see this" clearly spoke an intelligence agent clutching a DVD in his hand. Corporal Hopper a tall well postured muscular man, with grey crew cut hair, a freshly shaved face, and a few battle torn scars stood responsively in front of the mid-twenties agent who delivered the disc with such enthusiasm, the likes of which his brutally objective based mind-set had no comforts for. Grasping the disc the corporal lent forwards putting it into the disc slot of the table top whose holographic images displayed the counties landscape in a spectacular illumines 3D model.

The images projected from the table instantly clearing the landscape and the CCTV footage from multiple cameras of the bank projected the majestic rescue of the hostages from the bank, clearly displaying Max both exiting and entering the shadows. "That's what the doc did with his special concoction the sneaky bastard" spoke the corporal, his facial expression blank but clearly trying to smile at this great artefact of information he has been enlightened with "get me that kid sergeant" he ordered grabbing the sergeants sleeve to focus his attention and pointing at the now enhanced picture of Max's face. "Listen up operatives, it's time to launch operation dark spear" The corporal continued, scanning the environment with his eyes to ensure everyone absolutely understood and took in his request. "Time to get back that serum" the corporal muttered with a newfound confidence of getting back what had previously alluded him.

Max spent the weekend training building his

strength and speed so that he would be better pre-pared for his next heroic escapade. Deciding to go for a job to finish off the evening Max headed to-wards town, it should be a six mile round trip from his home, and due to his greater fitness he hoped to finish in around thirty minutes. The sky began to darken as the sun began to perch on the clouds in the distance, ready to sink into the horizon and leave a resounding darkness in its wake. A mild breeze gently brushed Max's cheeks as he ran, focused and controlled, pacing himself so as to achieve the tar-get he had set for himself. Black SUVs were situated near the corner of every single block of houses he passed, there windows darkly tinted as black as the paintwork itself, Max glanced back and recognised that they were all in fact the same model vehicles, "Whats going on?" he wondered, only allowing a meagre amount of concentration to answer the question so as not to lose his crystal clear focus.

"What the f.." Max yelped, leaping to slide across the bonnet of an SUV that had skidded to a halt so as to entrap him. The doors swung open, suited men exiting with pace, armed with tasers and electric looking batons. Max sprinted, the focus now gone, his thirst for beating the 30 minute target, left alone with the driver of the vehicle that so nearly hit him. They pursued him, sprinting to keep up with the illusive teenager they were for some reason hunting. "Block the road" screamed one agent chas-ing him, into the small microphone dangling by his neck from the earpiece he wore. Three more SUVs skidding in to block the road ahead, the rubber of their tires shredding as they forcefully skid to a halt leaving a path of smoke in their wake, more suited men exiting the vehicles rapidly. "Oh shit" muttered Max, both ways now blocked with people who clearly want to subdue him, "where can I go? Where can I go?!" he pleaded looking for a shadow or an escape route, anywhere to be rid of the caged trap that was closing down on him.

Terraced houses lined either side of the road, no alleyways or instantly recognisable exits presented themselves to Max. "Ohh no no nooo!" yelled Max diving head first through the single glazed window of number forty-eight, rolling into their front room as the elderly inhabitants sat eating their dinner and watching TV, "I'm sorry" Max shouted, scrambling through the house and escaping through the back door into the garden. Bang, the suited men kicked through the door in pursuit of Max, one lingering to pay the shocked couple left whose home was now swamped with suited men steaming through to capture their target.

Vaulting over the rear fence at the rear of the garden, Max was greeted by a Rottweiler hurtling towards him, the intruder in yet another strangers garden, its fangs bared ready to tear him limb from limb. "Whoops" he yelled, climbing onto their shed and leaping from there onto the roof of the houses outside single floor extension. Quickly climbing onto their tiled roof frantically as he glimpsed over his shoulder to see the abundance of agents swarming towards him. "Get him now, shoot, shoot" yelled the leading agent, his colleagues removing their tasers and directing them towards Max, "There!" Max spots a shadow just big enough in the next door neighbours garden as he scrambles across the rooftop trying not to slip on its tiles, diving off hoping to hit the shadow he had spotted. The clacking of the tasers as fifty thousand volts surged down them frazzled in the air as they each missed their target, except one capturing Max's ankle as he descended through the air for the shadow its hooks pinching into his skin, flowing with the extreme voltage which immobilised Max's body as he descended closer and closer to his freedom.

The excruciating pain surging through every muscle causing his body to involuntarily twitch and curl as he begged to hit the shadow and not the cold hard concrete beside it. His body now disappearing from view Max had done it luckily, he hit the shadow, his body still sore from the taser he no longer felt the voltage surging through as it couldn't enter the realm. The darkened surroundings now befriending Max even more, having saved him yet again from a terrible fate, Max watched intrigued at the identity of the people following him, who now grunted angrily at losing their target. The lead chaser now on the phone, Max moved closer to eavesdrop, "Corporal Hopper, it's Baker Sir, he got away" spoke the man, his expression now showing more fear of the reaction and punishment he would receive than the anger of missing his mark. A deeper, husky voice screamed down the phone, so loudly Baker had to distance it from his ear in an attempt to hear something being spoken with clarity. "How the bloody hell can forty of my top agents not capture a bloody teenager, you bloody disgraces!" the voice screamed, clearly hosted by a violently tempered man. "Fine that stupid kid wants to play hide and seek then flush the fucker out! Newspapers, TV, radio, social media whatever it takes!" the corporal continued, in a less brutally aggressive yet still adamantly authoritative voice. "Yes sir" Baker replied, before hanging up the phone "Come on then you useless sacks of shit!" he bellowed at his colleagues, clearly rebounding his superior's aggression onto his comrades, and with that they swiftly fled the scene. Max rushed to his local library, remaining in the shadows until he reached the shadow behind the tree opposite his home away from home, where he had repeatedly felt himself as he grew up, he re-entered the real world and crossed the road into the library hoping to do some research on the free internet access computers within.

An hour passed as Max frantically searched the internet for any military units that wear black suits, but only ended drawing up loose legend like stories from various conspiracy sites. Thinking back he remembered the corporal's threat and quickly checked the news website, his face stared back at him from the news frontpage, "Exposed chemically diseased contagious escapee on the loose" was the title of the story he quickly clicked to read more. "Oh shit... no no nooo" he began, reading the imaginary plot behind Max's supposedly chemically altered contagious virus style disease, and wanting more information on his name or whereabouts for a ten-thousand pound cash reward! "I'm screwed," Max said resting his head in his hands. Dated only thirty minutes ago Max paused for a second, before bounding from his seat panicking "I need to get home! Mum!".

CHAPTER 7: YOU'VE MADE IT PERSONAL

Max stood before his home, his eyes scanning the properties exterior frantically for any movement he may see through the properties windows but met with the disappointment of a motionless static scene. His eyes meticulously bounced between each window of the property a hopeless sense of despair growing with each glance. "No, no, please no...!" Max murmured charging towards the front door of his home which was left open and ajar. "Smash", the doors glass shattered as Max swung it open, hurtling his body inside.

"Please, please, please..." Max pleaded, charging through the house, finding only the demolished inners of each room that had been maliciously ruined, in such a fashion to resemble the burglary scenes from Max's favourite program; CSI. "Mum!" Max screamed in desperation, whilst standing eerily motionless in the lounge, anxiety ringing in his voice which echoed through the vacant property.

"It's all my fault" Max whispered, dropping to his knees, the hopelessness of despair lingering in his voice as he contemplated his worthlessness and failure to protect his family, the mother he loved and cared for throughout his life, who for no fault of her own is now a hostage to whoever destroyed his home.

Max's hands collided with the floor, one after the other in rapid succession as he screamed in rage frantically punching the floor beneath him. "You want me, you want my power, and you have taken me family!" Max roared pummelling the ground harder and harder, "You have made this personal!" he yelled, stopping his flurry of punches. Raising his head slightly Max's eye line connected with the reflective laminated surface of a DVD case labelled 'Max'. His heart fluttered, before increasing its beat as Max scrambled from the floor to grasp the clue before his eyes, taking the disc and inserting it into the TV's built in DVD player hoping for a clue to his mother's whereabouts.

"Hello Max!" Spoke the deep, authority sounding voice of the man Max could see on the TV screen. The man's muscular frame stood bolt upright with a religious like posture, his grey hair cut short in a military fashion which sat above his frowning face. His war torn skin, scarred and leathery, only highlighted further by the green military uniform he wore, badges sitting securely on his chest and ranked stature marked on the fabric of his shoulders. "If you are watching this, I assume you have by now come to the realisation that we have taken something of yours, which would seem to be an action you should be all too familiar with!" spoke the man, ending his sentence abruptly.

The man's eyes seemed to penetrate the screen with which they were projected from, as he seemingly stared at the viewer, Max. "Where are my manners..." the voice spoke more softly, as he began to pace from side to side on the camera. "I am corporal Hopper, the highest ranked member and leader of a military research programme called DarkScreen..." momentarily pausing to contemplate how much information he disclosed to Max. "We are a top secret military unit focused on human enhancement for military, strategic purposes, and the formula running within the blood in your veins is property of us!" He spoke, the frustration of Max's seeming capture of his formula aggravating him further.

"Long story short kid! You have something of mine, and now I have something of yours!" he yelled, a smirk all too similar to James, stretched across his face as he grabbed and pulled another person into the frame with such brutal force that their limbs flailed resembling a rag doll. "Say hello to mummy!" the corporal spat viciously with a clear smugness at the genius of his plan. "No!" Max yelped, tears welling in his eyes as the despair of failure sunk to the pit of his stomach causing nausea unlike anything he had felt before.

The figure that had been manhandled into the cameras view was Max's mother; her mouth bound with fabric, her hands tightly tied together behind her back, tear stains where makeup had run marked down her face and a terrified expression of fearful horror projected from her eyes in such a way they felt like they were penetrating Max's soul. "I am a reasonable man... I will give you until nineteen hundred hours today to come and hand yourself in at unit 42 of the dockyard, otherwise the head of your beloved mother will be in with tomorrow's mail in the post!" The voice bellowed, as the screen which went to static and the picture was lost. Max was frozen in a statue like fashion as the shock of the scenario that had unfolded before his eyes began to sink in. The image of his mother's fearful face scorched into his mind, as he reflected on what he had just witnessed and the threat that had been made. Max raised himself to his feet, adrenaline now seeping into his bloodstream as he became more and more conscious and unstuck from the hopelessness he was previously bound by. "You've taken my mother... I'll take your life!" Max grunted, marching furiously towards the exit of his house.

Staring whilst dormant, Max scanned the front of the pier with his eyes, tallying the visible defences that the corporal had opted to enforce as protection for the potential oncoming attack Max would undoubtedly action. Five miles, effortlessly sprinted through within the shadow realm with no apparent hindrance to his physical performance due to his increased endurance gained via the consistent chemical release of adrenaline into his bloodstream. Max looked down from his target to his hands which since leaving the shadow realm had begun to shake uncontrollably as his rage grew more and more the closer he got the prison of his captive mother.

"Eleven guards" Max chuckled, confidence gleaming through, almost offended at the lack of defensive security Hopper had initiated. Max stood in the darkened passage between semi-detached properties situated opposite the entrance to the port, the obviousness of unit 42 apparent by the ten foot barbed wire fences surrounding the compound, armed guards patrolling the interior proximity of the fences meant to prevent unauthorised people from being able to access the large forty-foot high warehouse structure positioned directly in the middle of the fences that surround it, with a single truck parked out front.

Max began to pump himself up by bouncing from one foot to another on the spot "Come on, come on, come on... Let's fucking do this!". Diving into the shadow before him Max entered the quiet solitude of the shadow realm he had now begun to appreciate, his rage growing considerably second by second as he played back the painful memory of the video within which his mother's captivation was so brutally cruel. Poised and tensed Max stood only metres away from the guards protecting the only entrance into the fort before him. "Maxxxxxx!" shrieked a woman, the pain in her voice echoing within Max's head almost paralysing him with the concern he couldn't help but feel, as he instantly recognised it to be his mother he was hearing. The source of the scream resonating from within a military armoured truck situated just to the front right hand side of the warehouse structure.

"You bastards!" Max screamed, plunging into the light of the shadows to reveal himself to the people to the real world, his fist raised punching towards the shocked guard who could only begin to turn his body to face his adversary. "Crunch" the punch connected with the side of the guards jaw , instantly dislodging it from its bound location on his face, two teeth pushing from between his lips to escape amongst the mouthful of warm blooding rushing to exit his mouth as he dropped unconsciously to the floor, crashing into it with the full force of his body-weight.

"Here!" screamed the guard hoping to grab the attention of his closest colleagues whilst raising the hand which now so desperately grasped the tasor situated in his sweaty palm, hoping to crimple his adversary. Max's focus was unbreakable, the momentum of his punch causing his body to spin on the spot, as he jumped up and raised his leg preparing to deliver an aerial roundhouse to the guard whose taser was now active, crackling loudly hoping to prevent his impending fate. The large man over six foot in height yelped loudly like a wounded child as Max's foot connected with his face, his nose shattering beneath the force of the foot that collided with it further snapping his head back in a whiplash causing motion before falling unstoppably into the ground beneath him.

Kicking the wire fence open with such force it snapped the lock holding it in place, Max leapt into the compound, the closer of the perimeter guards charging towards his exact location. From his previous recon before engaging in the attack Max had figured the exact whereabouts of the eleven guards; One in each corner of the compound, two at the front gate (now eliminated), one in front of the armoured truck, and two at the back of the truck, as well as two guards at the units entrance. If his attack goes according to plan then he will be fighting no more than two people at a time, by the time they are able to reach him.

Lunging forward Max thrusts his fist into the first accessible guards mid section, the moist spray of spit landing on his face as the air is forced out of his victims lungs, creating a mist in the night's cold air. The impact sends the guards limp body crashing backwards into the trucks door and springing off onto the cold hard concrete below with a loud thud. The impending footsteps and crackling of their tasers were the only noises echoing around the otherwise deserted docks.

Looking left and right Max needed to decide which of the two guards attacking each side would he engage first... Opting for the smaller of the two incoming from the right Max turned to face him head on, the guards arm drawn back with the taser ready to be brandished at him. Pacing forwards Max stopped, his reflexes kicking in once again as he grabs the incoming guard by the scruff of his collar, and using the guards momentum to assist Max rolled onto his back from standing, his feet pressed against the bewildered guards hips and his hands still tightly clasped on his collar, he continues to roll and then releases the collar whilst kicking out his legs slingshotting the guard into his colleague who had just reached them. Both bodies collided with a thunderous crunch shortly joined by multiple groans of pain by both of the debilitated bodies.

Rising to his feet, the two guards from the back of the truck and the two from the front of the building finally surrounded Max, "Nowhere to go kid" one of them grunted smirking as he did. "Whose first?" Max chuckled, confidence projecting from him even though he was outnumbered and out sized by his larger opponents. Faking a step forwards so the guard opposite hesitated waiting for the attack, Max lent forwards, his head almost touching the ground as he kicked out his right leg with the same motion of a donkey kicking, his foot impacting underneath the chin of the unsuspecting guard behind Max, lifting him inches from the floor before smashing back down to earth again.

Transferring his weight in a gymnastic fashion Max used this kick to propel himself into a forward roll, kicking out both legs simultaneously once flat on his back. Each foot reaching its target, pounding the shins of the guard in front of him, taking away his centre of balance as he now falls towards the smaller acrobatic teen that is swiftly disabling his team. Looking up at the giant descending upon him, the harsh glow of the distant floodlight becomes blocked as his large body casts a shadow swallowing Max just in time. Without the cushioning of the smaller adversary to break his fall, the plummeting guard faceplants the unforgiving concrete rendering him instantly unconscious with a shuddering smack.

Rolling twice to his right hand side Max was now behind the guard that was previously behind him, rising from the shadow he casted Max uppercutted the guards groin. An eardrum popping scream shrieked from the large man who dropped to his knees curling forwards in pain as he gasps frantically trying to suck in air despite his agonising pain. Now fully risen from the shadows Max stood tall behind the injured guard, his eyes locked with the last remaining guard whose face showed an inherent amount of both surprise and fear as his team had been disbanded before his eyes with relative ease and professionalism from a teenager! Max's face tightened as his brows curled into a frown, fury still surging within his veins as he prepared to disband his next victim.

Leaping onto the kneeling guards shoulder with his left foot Max propelled himself upwards towards the guard opposite, using his teammates shoulder as a step for his propulsion. Like a deer in headlights the guard remained frozen not even raising his hands to defend as the teenager hurled through the air towards him, fist raised. Crunch! Max's hand collided with the guards temple, his full bodyweight stacked behind the punch whipping back the guards neck who slammed into the ground.

"Max help" screamed his mother's voice instantly recognisable to Max, who turned his head quickly towards the source of the pleads for help, the truck. Sprinting past the front of the truck, whose door he had removed earlier with the assistance of the guards body, Max heard murmurs of what he could only assume were the two guards his recon had spotted behind the stationary vehicle. "Mum!" yelled Max, grabbing for the handle protruding from the back right hand corner of the truck's rugged exterior, its cold metal surface subjected to all Max's weight as his hands grasped so tightly his knuckles turned white. His airborne body pivoting around the handle both feet raised to dropkick the closest guard with the full power of his momentum. The velocity as his feet connected with the guards mid section threw the guard backwards so hard his colleague was wiped out as collateral. Both feet once hit the ground one after another as Max rips open the rear door and leaps into the truck "Mum?!".

The trucks inners were empty, Max scoured around the interior with his eyes as quickly as possible, the interior consisted of tiled metal sheets similar to those found in the kitchen of a commercial restaurant, nothing standing out at all. Standing confused but still certain he heard her voice come from within Max bellowed from the pit of his stomach "Mummmm!". His voice echoed throughout the steel chamber he now resided within, Max swung his hand hitting the trucks side in frustration. 'Click' a small noise came from the floor, looking down Max saw a tile had popped open, raising one side to be higher than the rest of the floor beneath his feet. Kneeling down to examine further Max pulled upwards on the tiles single raised edge to reveal the dark drop within "a trap door" Max whispered to himself. Pausing momentarily; somewhat fascinated by seeing a trap door in real life as opposed to just within the video games he frequently played, Max leapt into the darkness in a Gung-ho manner.

"Clang", both feet hit the floor beneath after a small drop into the darkness, Max's eyes struggling to adjust as the only source of light into the space was through the hole he had just dropped from. Total darkness engulfed his sight, as the trap door slammed shut, panic started to rise in Max as his breathing became shallower and faster as the reality of the situation began to sink in. Stepping forward cautiously he reaches out, his hand pressing against what feels like a smooth glass like surface.

"Hello Max", a cold, stern voice filled the room, sending a shiver down Max's spine as the realisation of being caught in a trap finally sinks in. A blinding flash goes off as the room is filled with a bright white light illuminating from the floor and ceiling whilst reflecting off the mirrors walls surrounding him. Not a single shadow in the room for Max to escape through, his hands clammy as he anxiously sweats pondering any other obvious kind of escape. "Nowhere to go kid... Nowhere to go" chuckled his captors voice through the speakers dotted amongst the ceiling lights. In a quick swift movement, the hatch in the ceiling is raised open and a taser is shot at Max piercing his left shoulder the loud crackle is followed by a whimper as Max's muscles twitch and he is sent paralyzed to the floor while the surge of volts work there way through his system until the light begins to fade passing to black as he goes limp, rendered unconscious.

CHAPTER 8: TRAPPED

Max's eyes are burning as he struggles any more than a squint, his head immovable as he wriggles to try breaking free from the straps he is held down with. As he becomes more and more alert Max can feel the various straps restricting his movement, around his forehead, neck, wrists, waist and feet. "Arghhh" he yells frustratingly, as he wriggles frantically trying to break free from his now claustrophobic situation. As his eyes adapted to the brighter light Max realised that he was either in the same room as before or one very similar to it, his eyes scanning the ceiling for the hints of the hatch he came in through but his eyes unable to focus clearly enough as the brightness of the lights burns his retinas becoming more and more unbearable the longer he struggles to keep them open. Tears seep down each cheek as the light is insufferable, his eyes fighting to reject it as though having dust within them, but failing miserably.

"So..." grumbled the voice he was now only all too familiar with, one of the mirrors panels scaling the sides of the room opened to reveal the silhouette of a tall well postured muscular man who entered before closing the door behind him. "You should know who I am by now Max, and we most certainly know who you are, in fact we know everything there is to know about you Max" spoke the Corporal, stepping forward and moving his face intimidatingly close to Max's. "But for the sake of good manners... I am Corporal Hopper" he spoke in a softer more accommodating voice moving back from Max's personal space again. "But make no mistake boy, this is not summer camp here, I hold all the chips, I am the master and the commander of this establishment and YOU are nothing but a thief! A mule harbouring military assets!" Hopper spat, his voice now harsher and unforgiving as he moves forward enough that his nose presses against Max's cheek as he bellows his statements.

Avoiding eye contact Max's heart was beating so loud it felt as though it was going to leap free from his chest, so loud he questioned whether the corporal could hear it as it drummed away in a rhythmic beat with a tempo so fast it resembled drum and bass as opposed to a regular heart beat. "W-Where's my mum?" he questioned innocently, so quietly that had the corporal not been close enough he wouldn't have heard. "They've been freed dear boy..." spoke the corporal, a smirk stretching across his battletorn face. "What have you done to them!" Max roared wriggling so frantically to break free of his constraints that he almost flipped the chair which he was strapped to. Stepping backward as though surprised by the sudden onset of rage displayed by the skinnier smaller teenager, Hopper grinned, the satisfaction in Max's despair evidently causing his happiness.

"Under the provision of complete secrecy with threat of execution governed by the military for espionage, your mother has abandoned you for her own freedom... the stupid cow even believed we would release you once the extractions complete... But you know too much now boy, prepare for a world of pain" grunted the corporal exiting the room once again. Max gulps as his mouth dries out of fear, the tight leather bound around his neck applying more pressure as he tries to swallow.

Hours pass, not a single noise or semblance of life has revealed itself to Max, whose frantic efforts to break free from the shackles that constrained him had failed so badly that he had all but given up on the possibility of breaking free from them. His skin sore and red where the friction of his attempts had burned through the top fragile layers of skin. "Come on! Come on you cowards! Get it over with!" screamed Max helplessly, unable to put up with the unbearable light which remained unrelenting as time passed. The lock of the door clunked seconds before it swung open, a shorter slimmer man entered, with long brown hair tied back in a ponytail, his white lab coat stained and tattered, and his eyes hollow as though looking into a soul-less abyss behind them. "W-Who are you? Get away from me!" yelled Max, wriggling more frantically to break free once again as he can't turn to fully see the entrant due to the restrictions strapping his head in place. Pivoting on the spot the man spun 180 degrees reaching back out of the doorway and pulling in what sounded like an old tea trolley, rattling as it moved, and its wheels squealing as though unlubricated for decades longer than they should have been serviced by. Max's eyes strained, peering out the corner of them trying to see the contents on the surface but too blurry to make out anything clear enough to identify.

"Who are you?! Please just let me go, I'm just a kid" pleaded Max, his request falling on seemingly dead ears as the room's other occupant looked at him in dismay before lifting a large needle from the trolleys surface. "Pleaseee!" cried Max desperately hoping to pull on any of the heart strings of his subduer. "Shut up!" barked the scientist frowning aggressively at Max, scanning Max's face as though trying to determine if diseased or safe. "I am Harkins, a scientist within the military research programme called 'Darkscreen'. We are a top secret military unit focused on human enhancement for military, strategic purposes" He continued, still looking warily at the boy. "Please, just let me go" Max begged as Harkins pierced his skin with the large needle he had previously brandished.

An intense burning sensation radiated from the injection, a stinging that seemed to pulse further and further throughout his body until not a single part of him wasn't seething in pain causing Max to squirm and shriek before once again blacking out. "Argh" Max gasps trying to sit up but unable to move still, the realisation that he had not woken from the nightmare he was living, sinking in once again as Harkins stops slapping his cheek, seemingly to reawaken the passed out teenager. "Come on kid, I expected more" chuckled Harkins who raised a pair of pliers from the trolley, "Let's see if we can't make you more comfortable eyy" he continued, his grin now stretching from cheek to cheek as the cold rusted metal of the pliers begun squeezing Max's skin, who yelped helplessly.

What felt like days had past, bruised, torn, bleeding and weak Max had been subjected to a routine of torture day after day. Unsure as to whether they aimed to extract the serum anymore or just sadistically enjoyed his suffering, perhaps both, Max thought, struggling to structure a clear thought pattern between the bouts of pain he was being subdued to. "Looks like you're going to have a new friend tomorrow" Harkins giggled in a somewhat schoolgirl manner, Max locked eyes with Harkin's unsure what he meant but without the energy to produce a sarcastic comeback.

The all too familiar clunk sounded just before the door opened revealing a larger more athletically built man with shoulder length pitch black hair hanging loose either side of his pointy featured face. "I am Aiden" he spoke after entering, his eyes scanning the weakened frame of the teenager before him. Max looking hopelessly towards him through the corners of his eyes, this man appearing kinder than Harkins, actually introducing himself before subjecting Max to the day's torturous events. Digging for more information Max queried the kinder Aiden hoping to get some much needed answers. "What is in me? How long till it's all gone? Will you let me go? Are you going to kill me?" Max splurted, pummeling his new company with a flurry of questions that were answered with nothing but a blank gaze from his new accompanying scientist. "Kid I can't tell you too much, the less you know the better" whispered Aiden, nervously glancing around the room as if they weren't alone.

"Please" Max begged, hoping for Aiden to reveal some of the information he is so obviously holding back. "You are the first successful human trial on a non adult..." Aiden started, leaning in so as to whisper even quieter than before, "There exists a realm beyond our own, a place in the shadows, a place which Darkscreen believes to hold a significant tactical advantage for the future of military operations." Aiden continued, pausing as he fumbled with the tools situated on the trolley, deciding which tool to inflict pain on his new acquaintance with. "It is rumoured that there is an order, an order which rules and protects the place we speak of, and they don't tell me much more, but with the bodies I have to identify postmortem, I can only assume they are resistant to anyone accessing it." Aiden finished, locking eyes with Max before plunging the needle into the protruding vein in his forearm.

Days past and Aiden wasn't seen again, Harkins had returned and was all too happy continuing to punish Max, who now was having vials of blood extracted daily, most likely for tests. The days turned into a blur, each one into the next as Max established weeks must have past by now, his emotions turned into an empty abyss of disdain no longer succumbing with weakness and cowardice when subjected to the ritualistic tortures each day, much to the distaste of Harkins. The walls must have been soundproofed, as the only noises heard each day were the clunk of the door lock, the rattle of the tools on the rickety trolley and the sadistic voice of Harkins.

Clunk, the familiar sound woke Max from his light sleep, his eyes opening to see the familiar blinding white light that scolded his retinas. The door opened, Harkins familiar scowl crossed the threshold into his chamber "Help me! Let me go!" a distant female scream shrieked in the distance just loud enough for Max to hear before the door slammed shut behind Harkins. "Mum?!" Max yelled, wriggling for the first time in weeks, his body stiff and sore from the non use of his muscles for such a long period of time. "You liar! Mum?!" Max continued spitting out in rage as Harkins smuggly locked eyes with him. "You really thought we'd let them go?" Harkins questioned his sarcastic manner making it difficult for Max to ascertain whether he was bluffing or not, but the emotional reactions were having an effect on Max's physiological state regardless. His blood started pumping faster and faster as Max could feel his heartbeat racing, adrenaline seeping into his bloodstream as his muscles tensed and growed due to the injection of power the adrenaline created.

"Harkins!" Max bellowed, his eyes locked in a staring contest with his captor whose face remained smug but also mildly concerned at the fact Max's will no longer seemed diminished and the leather bindings holding him creaked as Max struggled to break free. "Harkins hair was down today, no longer in the usual scruffy ponytail Max had become accustomed to, its coarse texture stroked Max's cheek as Harkins got right up in his face before whispering "Aww mummys gonna die..." his sentence was cut short "No!" screamed Max in fury, his eyes locked on the shadow the loose hanging hair of harkins was casting. A water like sensation rushing through his body propelling him from the restraints he had previously felt restricted by, his body no longer solid and physically objected to the realities of the physical plane as he swept from the chair into the small shadow he had been so intently focused on before.

The usual dark surroundings encapsulated Max, "What just happened?" he queried, uncertain of how he seemingly evaporated into a dark like fog flying him into the tiny shadow Harkins hair had created. The tiny light from Harkins, where the shadow had been disappeared as he pulled his hair back into a ponytail, the grunts of surprise shelled out through the array of swear words he spat so quickly in Max's disappearance.

"Mum", Max spluttered, his focus redirected away from the how's of the previous situation and returned to what motivated him to manage the feat in the first place. Charging through the door and down the long corridor Max saw another scientist entering a doorway on the right accompanied by two guards, one infront and one behind them, the shriek of "Nooo please" whistling through the hallway as Max takes off in a sprint to rescue her. the bank style vault door slamming shut just before he could reach it even with the assistance of his increased speed within the shadow world. Punching the door he yells in fury, the all too familiar scuttling as his rage had alerted the spider occupants once again to his presence within this realm. "Shit" he muttered stepping through a smaller light beside him and out of the shadow within the real corridor he was now alone in.

Looking back towards the room from which he had escaped whose door remained closed with Harkins still inside. The large vault door towered above

Max, who examined its surface, noticing a biometric scanner settled in the centre of its rugged exterior. "I need to get in there," he thought, his mind racing with both panic for his Mum and fear of recapture again. "You!" the familiar voice from his right spat as Harkins stood door ajar glaring at the smaller stature of Max who gulped deeply.

CHAPTER 9: FROM HUNTER TO HUNTED

T he cool breeze swept past Max's cheek as he parried a punch from Harkins who had charged at him. A barrage of punches followed, beating the air harshly as Harkins continued his attempts to strike the teen he had already gained so much pleasure from harming. Max's cool composure remained throughout, his MMA training now instinctual as muscle memory assisted in him slipping, ducking and rolling under the attacks of his tormentor. Each attack's power growing visibly weaker and weaker as Harkins breathing progressed from deep grunts to shallow puffs of despair as he continues being unable to strike his target.

A desperate haymaker... Made all too obvious by the loading of weight into his hips as his shoulder dipped ready to thrust his final hopeful punch at Max. Max breathed deep and calm, shuffling forward one step and twisting his hips as the punch was launched, grasping Harkins wrist with both hands as he pressed his hips into his midriff, using Harkins own weight and momentum to assist in throwing him with maximum power and efficiency into the solid ground they stood on.

A deep groan and gasp for air hurled out of Harkins mouth as he lay back flat on the floor looking up at Max who still had his wrist tightly gripped. "I should end you" growled Max twisting Harkins arm so that he is forced onto his front via a shoulder, elbow and wrist lock being tightly squeezed by who had been his victim for more than a fortnight. "But I'm better than that" Max whispered in his ear, releasing his arm in exchange for a tight squeezing vice around Harkins neck as he clutched on squeezing harder and tighter as Harkins struggled, until he twitched and then became limp and deadweight. "Sleep, you asshole" Max grinned as he released Harkins, somewhat satisfied in a small amount of revenge whilst remaining dignified and not dropping again to another person's level as he had done with James.

Max returned to his feet, standing over the now snoring, scruffy, limp scientist that laid out on the floor in front of him. "Let's see if we can't open this door eyy?" Max chuckled, pulling the limp body of Harkins across the floor and pressing his thumb into the biometric scanner. Clunk, the familiar sound rang like a bell of victory in Max's ears as the latch on the vault door sprung open allowing him to pull it open. The room was seemingly empty other than a small statured girl curled up and shackled to a rusty metal bed frame bolted to the floor. A long blue medical curtain hanging from the ceiling shielded more of the room from Max, but also aided in keeping him out of sight from the 2 guards and scientist he knew must be on the other side of it. Max was both surprised it wasn't his mum and disappointed, but at the same time felt a longing to assist this weakened girl who he knew had most likely been subjected to the same torturous routine he had been forced to endure.

The frightened girl had stopped screaming upon seeing Max, her body rigid and stiff as she gazed at him stopping her frenzied movements, tear stains decorated her cheeks as did bruises and needle marks on her arms. Her pale blue eyes glazed over somewhat as she stared in a daydream like manner at her potential saviour, blinking harshly as though expecting to re-open her eyes and no longer see him there. Max slowly raised his finger to his lips gesturing "shhh" to her, she nodded back at him in compliance as he moved slowly and quietly towards her, his eyes focused on the silhouettes of the 3 occupants behind the curtain who continued murmuring about the canteens poor selection of food choices.

"Test subject: 64937" read the clipboard hanging at the end of the frame, "how many of us are there" Max thought, standing up taller as he quietly attempted tugging on the chain on the girl's left wrist.

Smash! A fist comes flying through the curtain rail with enough velocity to send shadowman flying through the air and back into the lobby crashing into the wall. Robotic motor noises followed by heavy stomps as the curtain rail is sent hurtling across the room. With his ears ringing Max lifts his head, looking up to see a large mechanised suit covered in mirrored panels with large spotlights dotted across its rugged frame. Through a small transparent screen Max could make out the instantly recognisable face of Corporel Hopper smiling in satisfaction as the suits fists clench and smash together. "You think you're special, come get some." spoke the Corporal, his voice repeating through the exterior speaker of the suit he sat encased within, gesturing for Max to attack him. The 2 guards standing alongside the scientist with their backs pressed against the wall as the girl lays motionless on the bed in a state of surprise like a deer in headlights but knowingly incapable of assisting Max.

Max rose to his feet, the adrenaline and rage expanding within him like a relentless fire burning furiously from deep within him ready to scorch, singe, burn and consume anything caught in its wake. "Where's my motherrr!" he bellowed, pushing off the wall and stampeding forwards towards the large frame before him, his fists clenched and eyes locked onto the small panel behind which the corporal's face was situated. No response came from the corporal, grinning with satisfaction as he witnesses the rage encapsulating Max because he doesn't know the answer.

Commanding the large armoured exoskeleton at will the corporal raises its arm across his body, swinging it powerfully down with precise timing so as to meet Max's face as he steps within reach. A metallic twang sounded followed by a groan and thud as the backhand connected with Max's distinctive face, lifting his feet from the ground and propelling his entire body towards the wall opposite to the one which the two guards and scientist remained pressed against. Max's limbs flailed as he bounced and tumbled across the wall ending face first in the corner against the unforgiving ground which did nothing to soften his landing.

Max's eyes were closed, his body sore, and bruised, his consciousness drifting in and out in addition to the floating white dots darting sporadically in his eyes as he struggled to undaze himself from the dizziness that last attack had produced. A shriek rang in his ears as the onlooking test subject girl sat on the bed submissively gripping her knees, her eyes closing periodically between prayers of hope for Max's wellbeing and victory so that she too may be freed from the confines of her cell. Max's breathes slowed, deepening, an aura of calmness soothing him as he slowly extends out each arm, pressing against the hard cold floor to push up his chest, lifting his chin to once again gaze back towards the corporal who laughed with a confident arrogance, realising he had greatly overestimated the under matched opponent he had seemingly expected more trouble from.

"I won't lie Max, I am a little disappointed..." Hopper spoke, a chilling calmness tinted with the legitimate disappointment ringing in his voice. Lifting his body Max now knelt before Hoppers suit, his legs prepped to spring like a slingshot pulled to maximum tension, his brow tightened frowning deeper and deeper, a dark steam like substance leaking from his shoulders evaporating away after being more than two inches away from his skin. Max began to groan aggressively in a similar pitch to a dogs growl, his muscles feeling like they are expanding as the fibres of his physical cells bond with dark sludge like substance the gas iis emitting from. The tightening expanded from his shoulders and down his arms not unlike an artificial armour manifesting itself from the initial patch it began at in the centre of his chest. Max's focus momentarily switches to the physical sensations of his skin tightening, after the discomfort of feeling with acute distinction the pain of each muscle fibre ripping due allowing for their expansion and fusion with the dark substance fighting into any and all gaps within each physical cell of his molecular structure.

Dropping his chin in a resemblance to exhaustion Max fell forwards onto his hands, his breathing shorter and shallower as the exertion of his transition takes his toll. His peripherals noticing the larger, darker makeup of his hands as he turns his attention to them. Standing slowly, all the while investigating curiously Max locks his eyes back with Hoppers "That's more like it" Hopper commented, looking at Max, whose physique appeared ,more filled, the muscles in his arms bulging inches larger than moments before with skin resembling that of a leather like material, looking thicker and tougher but only apparent on each arm whilst his face remained gaunt with its usual pale complexion. Both Max and Hopper noticed Max's fingertips, once again having become the claw like structure that he had brandished before in the shadow world.

Max wearily stepped closer to Hopper, an intense focus in readiness should he be subject to another attack, Hopper didn't disappoint. Pulling back his suit's right arm, Hopper pivoted launching a straight punch once again towards the bleeding face of his adversary. slipping left of the attack Max felt the rush of wind as the punch passed, pivoting around so now angled to his opponent Max swung his left claw. The pointed nails passed easily through the thick armoured plating on the Hoppers midriff, leaving deep ripped tears that exposed the now cut skin of Hoppers physical body situated beneath the armoured plating he had so happily hidden behind. A deep grunt of aggravation echoed through the speaker of Hoppers suit, the wound having only angered him further.

Hopper leaps towards Max unleashing a flurry of

attacks, hooks, straights, uppercuts, backhands, a relentless untiring barrage of attacks forcing Max's back to the wall as he struggles to duck, dive and dodge, each time narrowly avoiding incoming attacks. Large chunks of concrete and mortar ripping from the walls as each punch punishes the wall behind where Max's face never stayed long enough to hit. Pushing off the wall for propulsion Max sprinted for the girls bed, narrowly dodging the wide overhand hook swung by the corporal, and sliding into the shadow under the bed as if tackling someone in a game of football.

Hopper turns around swiftly, his metal frame stomping as he angrily stomps his foot, "come back here you little shit!" he roared. The metal clunk followed by the noise of a gas release as a metal plate on each arm releases, propelling a robot sized combat knife and a robot sized taser pole into each hand of his exoskeleton. The crackling of the taser hissed throughout the room, the air around the taser popping as it reacts to the electric pulses being emitted. Max stood up staring at his adversary from the safety of the shadow plane, examining its structure looking for any points of weakness whereby he could disable the suit rendering the Corporal marginally harmless, at least a lot less harmless than he could be.

"I know you're still there Max!" The Corporal hissed confidently, "You wouldn't leave your fellow abomination behind now would you" he chuckled stepping beside the bed frame which the terrified girl sat on, the razor edged combat knife raised to rest against the delicate looking skin on her cheek. "Either you come back now, or her blood is on your hands!" he bellowed, the girl whimpering as she fears her potential impending demise. Max's heart began to race, pounding faster and faster as he battled between the potential guilt of leaving her in order to guarantee his own freedom, vs his anger at the Corporal for kidnapping his family, having him tortured and threatening a seemingly harmless girl.

The corporal draws back his arm to strike with the blade, "Nooo" Max screams sliding back through the shadow he had previously escaped through, his thin body sliding out through the gap between the legs of the exo suit which stood wide stanced beside the bed. The corporal glanced down quickly realising he had just missed Max who rose to his feet quickly thrusting his shadow entrenched claw deeply into the raised bevelled box on the suits back armour plate. Gripping, squeezing and pulling as hard as physically possible Max's hand ripped free from the suit where his claws had so easily passed through, a handful of wires clasped firmly in his grip as the suit slumps, its lights going out as it appears the power down. Sharply turning his head towards the two guards and scientist with a menacing glare they evacuate hastily through the still open vault door, their footsteps quietening as they progress down the corridor away from Max.

A flush of happiness passes over the test subjects face, for the first time Max gazed at her smile, knowing his decision was the right one to come back for her. Stepping calming around the side of the now paralyzed suit Max used the sharp tips of his claws to pass through the armoured glass behind which the annoyed Corporal was shielded, drawing a circle so that a piece fell forward clattering on the ground exposing the man which had caused so many people distress. "This isn't the end you little..." The corporal started, his sentence stopped short as Max's fist thrusts through the small circle cut out he had just made, impacting his older opponents face with such force he is rendered instantly unconscious, the entire mechanized suit tumbling backwards to crash onto the hard floor beneath them.

Using his claw one last time before transitioning back to his normal human form, Max cut free the restraints the girl had been bound by. Sitting down slowly onto the bed beside her he softly asked "What's your name?". "Anna" she replied, her voice soft and innocent, as she stares gratefully at Max, "where did you go? How did you disappear?" she questioned warily, not wanting to interrogate her saviour. "I went into the shadow realm..." he answered, quickly following with a question of his own "What can you do? It says test subject, have they given you a power?".

Reaching out timidly Anna places her hand on Max's hand, her palms slightly warm as sweaty from the recent stress of the scenario she has just been encompassed by. Her eyes transitioned into a complete darkness, becoming pitch black as Max gazes into them "Thank you for saving me... I thought I might die in this place" Max hears, noticing that her lips hadn't moved. Max being the comic book fanatic he was, realises her ability straight away, telepathy on touch. "Your welcome" he answered, rising to his feet and pulling her up by her hand as he stands "we need to go," he muttered, making for the hallway from which they had come.

Stopping to breath Max and Anna panted, "this place is like a maze," she gasped, as the pair had seemingly ran through a variety of corridors and doorways without seeing another person, window or exit. Max's heart pounded quickly, the rhythmic beat synchronizing with the incoming footsteps he could hear getting louder and louder the other side of the double doors behind which they stood. Ushering Anna back, they stood clear of the door momentarily hesitating in taking off as to not draw attention to their location, running on the assumption that their exact location wasn't yet known.

The footsteps stopped, moments passed slowly, time seemingly stopping as Max gestured to remain silent to Anna would stood frozen and immobilised as an uncomfortable anxiety filled atmosphere filled the corridor they now stood within. Max's eyes remained locked on the shiny chromatic surface of the door handles, hoping for them not to turn. Not unlike a sixth sense Max felt a shiver crawl up his spine as he pushed Anna backwards yelling "Run" to her at the same time as the doors exploded open via a door charge whose remnants along with splinters of the door frame were launched into the corridor. The small framed girl took off along the corridor taking the second available door on the left as Max remained, ready to buy her some time.

"Move, move" a deep voice grunted as what Max assumed were multiple people entered the hallway which he remained within. The quantity of people undeterminable due to the multiple floodlights held projecting at him, there brightness scorching his retinas in a familiar way to those of the lights above his torture zone. The heat radiating from the lights began to burn Max's skin as they moved closer, stepping forward ready to engage in combat two of the lights part, the reflections from the metal ball only noticeably glistening split seconds to late just before it collided with its target. Max's knees hit the ground hard as he drops forward, gasping for air which had been forced from his lungs by the metal ball now being dragged away from him by its attached chain, screeching as it rubs against the concrete floor beneath.

It felt darker down on the ground, Max thought who looking forward was able to identify four sets of feet in front of him, a snigger sounding from behind the hum of the powerful lights. "Finish this now" that same deep voice commanded, followed by the metallic swipe sound Max knew to be a blade being unsheathed.

Rubbing his hands slowly along the floor he now knelt on Max grabbed a the larger of the sharp splinter fragments that remained from the exploded door. The piece of wood around two inches long, and still felt warm to the touch as multiple embers glowed along its edge. A pair of black boots stepped closer to Max's side, a silhouette of the man before him was the only visible characteristic as the lights continued to hinder Max's vision. Raising his hands as though to cower and plead Max faced the assailant, his weapon tucked away from view hidden by his palm as he prepared for his moment. "You're only going to get one chance Max, do this right" Max thought, plunging the weapon wielding hand down towards the floor with as much velocity as he could manage.

"Argh" a shriek came from the man as the pointed wooden piece penetrated the boot on the top of his foot piercing the soft flesh that sat behind it. Max felt a steady burst of warmth spread across his hand as blood projected from the deep wound as Max snatched his weapon free from its source. The wounded assailant hopped sideways clutching his foot just as Max had hoped him to. His movement overlapped one of the floodlights, casting a small but visible shadow where his body partially blocked the light. Falling sidewards from his knelt position Max slipped into the now refreshingly comforting environment of the shadow realm, the darkened area and long entangling webs slung across almost all surfaces no longer scaring him.

"Not so quick!" grunted the exuberated man rising from beside Max who now scuttled backwards. "How? How the hell are you here? What are you?" Max gasped, the true fear of how the man had followed him into the shadow realm horrifying him. The other three men following him into the realm, grinning profusely at the obvious surprise Max's face displayed. "There's no running from us" smugly spoke the smaller of the four men, all moving as a pack to surround their prey. Knowing that his chances for victory are slimmer than ever before Max paused momentarily, thinking strategically for his best odds for escaping or surviving this encounter.

Raising his fingers to his mouth Max whistled loudly in a summoning tone not unlike when cowboys would call across a horse in the old western movies. The familiar echoes of scuttling started in the distance, as Max had hoped for, planting his feet and pushing the hunter in front of him to give him a location to lunge for freedom. A fist flew in from both the left and right assailants, ducking to dodge the first strike Max was caught by the second, his face pulsating as blood poured down from the fresh cut above his right eye. The taste of iron lingering in his mouth as blood crept into the corner crevices of his mouth, leaving the familiar dissatisfying metallic taste at the back of his throat. The opponent in front having regained his footing after Max's push, kicked out towards the dazed teenager before him. Catching and locking the foot as taught throughout his MMA training Max swept the remaining foot sending the assailant crashing onto the ground.

The scuttling having now grown loud enough it could easily be mistaken as a worker digging a hole with a pickaxe, albeit with the rapid tempo even a group of workers would fail to maintain. Having flattened his first opponent Max had a clear view of the darkened horizon the silhouette of a giant arachnid speeding towards them. The shadow hunters understandably could hear the noise but remained unfazed and focused on their prey with a laserlike focus undetering regardless of anything that may distract a less encompassed person. "This is it" Max thought to himself, a small sense of optimistic hope growing within him as the large eight legged creature was now in range pouncing forward with its pincer like teeth prepared and a high pitched squeal projecting from it. Max squatted quickly in preparation, the arachnids multiple eyes all locked on the smaller of the five people within its realm, most likely with the trepid anticipation of at least catching the smaller prey before pursuing a larger target that appears more physically capable of getting away.

"Ahhhh" Max screamed, thrusting his shadow form as high as physically possible, tucking his knees into his chest, the desperate shriek surprising the shadow hunters who only then re-aligned their focus from their target to the large creature propelling itself through the air towards them. Whilst upside down in mid rotation of his backflip, higher than he had ever achieved before, Max's hair brushed along the back of the spider who narrowly passed beneath him. With its legs outstretched all but the already downed of the shadow hunters were sent tumbling to the ground, the one previously stood behind Max taking the brunt of the force had travelled close to five metres away from where he had been stood milliseconds before.

Max's feet hit the ground softly turning his head back towards the creature which may just choose to pursue him once again. A glimmer of red caught his eye, the first bit of colour he had seen in this realm which he believed only capable of manifesting black and white. Looking down towards the distant red which stood out so distinctly against the monochrome backdrop, glistened a ruby like gem enclasped within a silver intricately engraved housing, seated on a silver linked chain that had been dulled by the dust as it hit the floor. "Noo" a voice of pure panic as the hunter who had been launched furthest patted his neck area aimlessly, his eyes darting across the floor beneath him rising to Max who stood over the thing which he seemed in despair of losing.

His brows closed to a deep frown, eyes locked at

Max's feet as he rose to his knee in a lunge like position preparing to stand as his hand reaches over his shoulder to behind his neck unsheathing a scimitar whose white glowing aura stopped around the outlays of the runic engravings along the blade. Max's eyes locked with his, the true desperation apparent through the atmospheric aggression the hunter now radiated as though this amulet was a live or die object without which he is dead. Max could see the dark outline of the spider rising as it stood tall to its original standing position behind the knelt hunter, ready to un-empathetically attack the unaware victim before it. Turning with a majestic force the blade of the hunter struck the spider's head, the hunter returning to the exact same knelt position as before whilst the front part of the spider face thumps off the ground completely detached from the body which crashed down moments after.

Max gasped, "this hunter's speed was incredible, the blade cut through the spider like butter... he's going to kill me!" Max thought, panic beginning to make his legs tremble as the other hunters returned once again to their feet. "Get my amulet" shouted the knelt hunter angrily pointing at the object. Max reacted quickly, panic and exhaustion no longer allowing him to contemplate the consequential outcomes of his actions as he stomped down into the glistening crystals surface shattering it in a small red puff of smoke, leaving only the silver housing and chain behind. "Nooo!" bellowed the hunter, reaching out and grabbing at the air before him as though to capture the essence of the amulet which had just been dismantled before him. "Thorak, return to the sanctuary and bring me back another! I can't be trapped here again!" roared the painfully angered hunter, almost growling towards Max with pure hatred as his colleague disappears back into the real world.

"Three versus one you prick, you're in for a world of pain" he grunted standing to his feet and removing another glowing scimitar from his back plate of armour so he clasped one in each hand. "Diee!" he screamed charging towards Max, the cool breeze kissing his face as the blades strike past one after another as Max dodged, ducked and weaved so none of the attacks hit their mark. The flurry steadying for a second as his colleagues stood and watched prepared to witness Max's decapitation in a short amount of time. Max began to notice that the attunement of his senses grew stronger and greater the longer he remained within the shadow realm, realising that this was the reason he was able to so narrowly avoid the clutches of the arachnids pincers. Max was no longer able to just hear the sound of the blades slicing through the air, he could feel the vibrations of the molecules splitting around the blade as it carved through them, his senses interpreting so much information with such clarity he begun to feel as though time was slowing when in fact he was just reaching the next level of awareness he had yet to achieve previously.

The echoes of scuttling once again filled the distant air but on a much larger scale, so much so that the quick vibrations were noticeable through the floor they stood on, as a horde of spiders broke over the horizon towards their dismembered comrade. Seizing the opportunity Max hopped backwards his body at a forty five degree angle as one of the scimitars cuts the fine hairs on his chest. Rolling backwards onto the floor Max's momentum flowed into his shoulders loading with tension that sprung him upwards and backwards his body following an arch in the air as flips mid arch so as to dive into the small shadow opening beneath him, his eyes just capturing the other shadowhunters unsheathing there glowing weapons ready to fight the army that stampeded towards them.

Max rose from the shadow just outside of the underground infrastructure he had been captive within for what felt like so long, blood still pouring from his face as a stark reminder that the injuries obtained within the shadow realm pass through into the living world. "I need some answers" Max panted, running back towards town.

CHAPTER 10: NOT ALONE

Weeks passed last hours as Max was stuck in a daze frantically reliving the events that had occurred before him. His body now physically healed leaving only scars as a reminder of his entrapment, but the mental cracks still openly visible to anyone who he reluctantly communicated with. He had returned to his home, his mother swearing that the Corporal was a sadistic liar that did not offer freedom in exchange for her son, yet Max's fragile mind was too tired to care whether she was telling the truth or not. "Max... It's time for dinner" softly spoke his mother who creaked open the door slightly so as to check her son. Max lay on his bed staring at the ceiling unresponsive to his mother's words as his mind replayed the same memory fragment of the shadow hunters repeatedly as though searching for an answer he may have missed. "Well it's here if you're hungry son" said his mother placing the tray with a roast dinner on it beside him.

Max returned to school, his mundane life continuing from where it left off as he drifted from class to class completely unenthused with the subjects which attempted to distract him from his investigation scribbling down notes and drawing small doodles of any and each detail he may have missed. "They followed me in! And had abilities and weapons for the shadow realm, but how?" Max thought, attempting to poke holes in the questions he had already asked himself over and over. "Earth to Max..." spoke Miss Finley, his Science teacher, a tall, slim middle-aged woman with chestnut coloured hair tied back into a bun that perched on the top of her head. Looking up Max locked eyes with his antagoniser "And, he's back in the room" she giggled, as his classmates sniggered at the dazed teenager. Opening the blind so the beams of bright sunlight shone into the classroom, Max looked up "That's it!" he said aloud, rising to his feet excitedly, a grin spread from cheek to cheek. "What's it?" answered Miss Finley staring at Max with an expression of utter confusion as he bolted out of the classroom door leaving her and his fellow classmates in a bewildered silence.

Charging through the hallways Max thrust open the libraries double doors, breaking the deathly silence as the crash echoed within the large hall like room. "Sshhh" hissed the librarian to the right, her head barely popping up from over the counter behind which she stood, scanning in all of the old books that had been returned and stacking them on a small rustic looking tea trolley beside her. "Sorry," Max whispered, pacing quickly towards the computer section of the library before sitting down and opening the search engine within his browser. Max sat staring at the blinking cursor unsure what to type as he mulled over the fragment that he had been reminded of in class by Miss Finley who wore a small delicate ruby on a dainty gold necklace which shimmered catching Max's eye as she opened the blinds. "What did he say about the Red Amulet?" Max questioned himself, remembering the shadow hunters' fear and resulting aggression when it was taken from him and the panic when Max smashed its red centerpiece.

"I'll be trapped here again... that's what he said" Max spoke aloud to himself once again, feeling the heat of the librarian's eyes burning in the back of his head as he knew she would be glaring at him. Max sat for another few minutes with a new plethora of questions entering his head, is it the source of their power? Is that the way they could enter the shadow realm? Is it magic or technology? Max paused and began searching the internet, for any mention of the shadow realm, magical amulets, superpowers, legends, myths, folklore, anything that could help him piece together some kind of background. But all his research drawing up blanks, nothing that he could use to give him the answers he so desperately longed for.

Slumping backwards to rest his full weight against

the uncomfortable chair he sat on Max glared hopelessly at the screen. The familiar "Sshh" hissed once again from the librarian as the doors clanged open with force clicking as they locked back into place. Multiple footsteps paraded towards Max's location stopping meters behind him once again allowing for the silence the library was accustomed to. "Hello again" spoke a gritty deep voice, Max instantly recognised from the continual replaying of his memories of them, shadow hunters. The shiiiii- ing sound of metal being unsheathed from its binding whistled in Max's ear as he spun on his chair to face those behind him. "You must leave this library at once!" bellowed the library, noticing that the attendants were not students at the school, "I will call the police..." she then commented in a softer more fearful tone as the smaller of the three turned and began pacing over to the desk.

That moment was all Max needed, his eyes darted from the brandished blade to the door, his escape plan. Pushing off from the desk behind him Max's chair rolled forward, his feet slamming into the ground as he stood tall, swivelling his body whilst clasping the back of the chair and in an elegant motion swinging it like a baseball bat into the weapon wielding hunter whose blade clanged on the floor followed by the thud of his body. With only one hunter left beside him Max charged forwards, nudging him aside as he charged for the door and took off down the hallway. The school bell rang to symbolize the end of class and students swarmed into the hallways funneling out from the classrooms in an unordered chaotic manner, "Move, move!" Max yelled frantically waving his arms as his three pursuers entered the hallway shortly after him. His fellow students parted to either side of the locker ridden hallway allowing Max to pass through, desperation clearly displayed on his face as he continued to glance over his shoulder ensuring his hunters were not gaining on him.

"Arghh" Max's ragdoll like body slammed into the ground, sliding along the floor as the momentum pulled him forwards. Looking backwards he could see the smug grin of James, whose foot remained outstretched as a confident reminder that he was Max's demiser. The three hunters ground to a halt, "Step aside, official government business" grunted the tallest of the three stepping forward in an authoritative manner so as to seize control of the crowd of students slowly growing around them. "You're not from here" James snorted, stepping forward in front of the hunters, much to the surprise of Max who realised that James' hatred for authority must overthrow his hatred of Max. A silence filled the air as the stand off continued, a small wall of teenagers separating Max from the predators which pursued him like prey they relied on to survive. "Smack" the loud sound rang in the hallway, as back of the hunters hand collided with James's cheek, making his head whip sideways quickly, "big mistake" James chuckled spitting blood on the floor "get out of here Max, if anyones gonna end you, it will be more" he grunted, pulling a knuckle duster from out of his pocket and punching his attacker dead on his nose, before his followers lunged for the remaining hunters.

"Thanks" Max gasped, rising to his feet and taking off down the hallway, not looking back, but completely overwhelmed by the fact that his arch enemy and all those that have made his life a living hell throughout the entirety of his school years have risen to his defense in his moment of need. Sliding to a halt in front of his locker Max frantically spun the lock entering his combination before launching open the door and diving into the shadows which sat within the locker space. Breathing quickly he looked around, once again the darkened surroundings eerily quiet but somewhat soothing for his shaken nerves. "They won't know where I entered, I will be fine, but how did they find me?" Max muttered to himself, querying the tags they may have had within the school system, or the infiltrators within the staff they may have, perhaps they could even have satellites tracking his movements. Max's mind wandered relentlessly but unable to ascertain a legitimately via option, he exited the school grounds within the shadow realm, still grateful to James who he began re-evaluating given the act of kindness he showed.

The school's reception doors swung open, creating a

crystal clear bang Max knew was on this plane. Spinning his head to be sure that an arachnid wasn't pursuing him Max's eyes set upon a much worse threat, the three hunters stood glaring at him, the red amulet on the center hunters neck hovering slightly and pointing directly towards Max's direction. "It's a tracking compass as well" Max whispered, allowing the excitement of more knowledge to briefly interrupt the ensuing danger he found himself in. "You can't escape kid, your ours..." the shorter member grunted, followed by the tallest of the three "dead or alive we only need 4 pints of your blood" he chortled with a joyful glee that made it apparent that only death would satiate the thirst they had.

Repositioning to face back toward the treeline he had previously planned on heading through, Max took off in a sprint, his shadow form dramatically increasing his speed and endurance as he took off much faster than any of his pursuers could follow. His heart raced not from the cardio he was subjecting his body too but instead from the surge of adrenaline that pulsed throughout his entire body causing the physiological changes he had experienced before; his skin darkening, claws forcibly extracting from his fingertips, a lightness in his body that allowed him to be more visibly agile skipping over the roots that protruded across the forest floor like a dense carpet of shrubbery. And the most noticeable quality he hadn't had the chance to fully appreciate in any previous encounters; his focus...

His senses were more attuned than ever before, every smell and sound fully describable with absolute clarity, and a tunnel vision encapsulating anything he gazed upon.

"He's getting away" a distant pant yelled, as the distance between Max and his pursuers continued to grow "Split, split now" another ordered, as the pack separated, the two hunters either side him diving into the light that returned them to the real plane of the living . Max neared the other edge of the forest, beyond the trees was darkness unlike within the forest which glowed beautifully due to the uncountable shadows cast by the branches overhead which illuminated his path. "If we can't have you, maybe we'll just pay mummy a visit" the remaining hunter snorted, his remark only audible due to the increased sensitivity Max's abilities enabled. Max halted instantly turning to face his antagoniser that continued towards him, slowing only when five metres before him. "Leave my family out of this!" Max roared, "This ends now!" he continued, unclenching his fists to reveal the claws he knew could dismantle his opponent. Raising his second hand to the hilt of his sword the hunter separated this single sword into two swords, both glowing with that same glittery shimmer "Come get some" the hunter confidently taunted. Both Max and the hunter paced sidewards in a circular motion resemblance of a shark closing in on its prey, their eyes locked in a tense staredown, each waiting for the other to launch an attack but neither willing to go first. Leaping forwards both swords swung in a pincer like motion at Max who rolled diagonally forward to his left, under and clear of the attack, whilst reaching out his claw to rip the flesh on the hunters right leg who let out a gasp of pain whilst rotating to face his younger opponent. Lunging forward Max swung his claw at the wounded hunter before him, withdrawing the claw slightly as he rotates low and kicks out his leg in a sweeping motion that wiped the hunters feet off the floor, leaving him prone on his back looking up at his impending defeat. "This ends now!" Max bellowed raising his right claw to strike the downed opponent and finish his prey who raised his sword's in a defensive cross stance to try and catch the downward swipe. "Now" he shouted, the hunter looking off to the side as Max felt a burning surge of pain around his raised hand's wrist which prevented him from continuing the motion required to finish his downward final blow.

"Argh" Max yelped in both pain and frustration as he glanced to see the glowing whip that had clasped tightly around his wrist, following the whip with his eyes to see one of the hunters which had previously separated during their hunt stood clasping the other end tightly with both hands. "Argh" once again that same painful sensation emanated from his other wrist which as he was distracted was an easy target for the remaining hunter that too had separated from the pack to reveal himself. Both hunters pulled so hard on the whips simultaneously that Max's arms were outstretched horizontally leaving him completely vulnerable as the remaining prone hunter rose to his feet, a grin spread from cheek to cheek as the pack's experience had once again snared them a target. Circling the trapped target, the hunter chuckled, mentally tormenting his prey, before kicking the back of Max's legs, knocking him to his knees, before completing the circle and standing before his kneeling soon to be victim.

"So kid, any last words?" the hunter queried, Max looking up helplessly didn't answer, but instead rose from his knees in a final defiant act who the hunter believed was an attempt of dying with honor. "Very well" the hunter hissed raising his sword to strike the final penultimate blow "noo" Max shouted, kicking off the ground in a manner that he ran up the hunters body and into a backflip whilst pulling his arms together sending both whip holding guards crashing into each other. Startled the sword wielding hunter leapt forward slashing towards Max who parried and allowed the blade to cut the whip which had held so tightly to him before, freeing his right arm which he quickly used to try and cut free his left arm with his claws but failing poorly.

"Smack" the loud bang echoed within Max's head, his ears ringing relentlessly as his vision fades to black and he tumbles to the ground. Max's eyes fought to stay open, as he dozed in and out of consciousness, as his limp body is dragged forward towards a large aged tree stump where they rest his head. The same scorching pain burned around his neck as they wrapped the glowing whip around it, each end held firmly by a hunter to restrain Max pressing his face into the splintered wooden stump where he was to be executed. "I've had enough of you now you little shit!" angrily ranted the lead hunter who joined together both of the swords he had previously separated, leaving him with a large thicker shining blade that will easily decapitate the petulant kid presented before him. Both hands tightly gripped the hilt as the hunter drew back the sword above his head for maximum power in his strike, "Time to die" he roared swinging down the blade swiftly as Max closed his eyes.

"Clang", the distinct noise of metal hitting metal rung in the air, as Max's head tilted to the side. Out the corner of his eyes he could see a pitch black crystalline looking blade resting above his head having prevented his death. The darkened blade led back to a decorated silver hilt that had been intricately carved with patterns and runic looking symbols, holding the blade was a large, well built, muscular creature. His skin was a tough snakelike texture, black the same as Max's had become, his long black hair swayed with the movement his block had created and his eyes glowed green, as though replaced with neon glow sticks. Max's eyes remained blurry as he struggled to keep them open as the creature struck out against the hunters, dominating them with a majestic ease as it moved fluidly with an acrobatic beauty that mesmerised his opponents. The fight continued around him as Max struggled to his feet, no longer bound by the whips which had appeared to have drained him of so much energy prior to being blindsided into a semiconscious state. Blinking, slowly Max's vision restored its clarity as he finally stood tall, his strength and feeling of stability slowly returning to him. "This isn't over" yelled the shadow hunter whose finishing blow had been prevented only shortly before, as he and his colleagues retreated back into the human realm.

The darkened man stood warily, his presence powerful and intimidating as he turned to face Max, his face moving to show a reassuring expression to the younger victim he had just rescued. "Who are you?" Max queried softly, "T-Thank you for saving my life" he continued gratefully, "I am Thorak" the figure spoke, his deep gravelly voice authoritative but kind, "come with me" he spoke as gesturing for Max to follow him, which he sheepishly did. Max walked beside Thorak with a cowering loyalty resemblant of a dog following its owner after doing something wrong. His eyes alternated in glances from the floor in front of him and looking in admiration at the larger male figure before him, "how did you know where I was?" Max asked sheepishly, locking eyes with Thorak who turned his head to face the boy. "Why did you help me?" Max continued before his original question was answered, "Are you human too?" he finished, stopping on the spot as Thorak halted and turned to face him. "You ask a lot of questions boy" he answered, the stern expression on his face turning into a small smile "curious one aren't you..." he chuckled, pausing to think about how he would articulate an answer to all Max's questions without divulging more information than he wanted to let out.

Before Thorak had a chance to answer the now familiarly haunting sound of scuttling thundered through the air as a pack of the overgrown spiders charged on their location. Looking quickly for an exit into the real world Max stepped towards a patch of light but was stopped by the firm grip of Thorak pulling him back by his forearm with a delicate force that once again demonstrated his immeasurable strength. "They'll kill us!" Max whimpered, shuffling so that he was now slightly behind Thoraks larger frame as a hopeful shield to prevent Max's imminent demise. The spiders descended closer and closer on their location, fifty metres away, twenty five metres away "we need to go" Max begged knowing it was too late and his fate was already sealed by the quantity of the pack. Thorak raised his arm, hand outstretched with his palm facing towards the spiders "No" he grunted, Max closed his eyes, and the scuttling stopped.

Max slowly opened his eyes as he felt Thorak's body moving away from him, frozen he looked all around him. "How?" he muttered, surrounded completely by the swarm of overgrown spiders that dwarfed him in comparison, all of which stood perfectly still. Max looked back towards Thorak who was now only a metre from the largest of the spiders face, his outstretched hand patting the spiders head in a rewarding fashion. "They obey you?" Max muttered still shaken by the near death he almost experienced again within that same day. "This is our ride..." Thorak spoke climbing up on the larger spiders back, "hop on one kid" he gestured towards the selection of spiders available that surrounded Max who remained frozen in astonishment for seconds before doubtingly mounting a spider to his right.

"This is insane, they tried to kill me" Max shouted across to Thorak, loud enough to hear over the loud scuttling sound surrounding them as Max clung tightly onto the spiders neck pressing his chest against its back so as to get extra reach to grip and hold on for dear life as the wind of motion pounded against his face. "These arachnids are protectors of the plane, alongside our kind" Thorak responded, his deep voice easily audible over the scuttling that attempted to drown out all other sounds. "Our kind" Max muttered quietly pondering if there are more like him, his eyes still locked on Thorak who nodded somehow having heard the whisper, he pointed to the distant horizon, Max's eyes followed the direction of his finger to see a large structure in the distance. As they got closer its features became more prominent, the old looking structure was built with a cathedral looking architecture. Its large arched doorway at the front was outlined with intricate carvings within its stone that looked like runic symbols unlike any Max had ever seen before. Three distinguishably separate towers protruded from the roof but were built closely enough together that from a distance they resembled a single turret. Large stone sculptures stood tall either side of the archway, both of these forms not too dissimilar in figure from Thorak and Max.

Max's eyes continued to scan the buildings exterior in more and more detail as they continued closer and closer to the structure until it was no longer a small distant building but a large compound that towered above them. "We're here" Thorak grunted dismounting from the arachnid, Max followed his lead dismounting and jogging to his side, pressing his palm against the three to four metres tall door Thorak forced it open gesturing to Max in a way to usher him inside as the arachnids scuttled off into the distance. The interior of the structure consisted of a large atrium, stairways from both the left and right met in the centre on what appeared to be a next level, another archway concealing the rest of the building from the lobbys view. The marble floor was shiny a perfect canvas to reflect light onto the ceilings intricately carved decorative ceiling that displays a tribal like pattern with intertwined runic symbols and captured small scenes of battles Max could only assume were trophies of monumental victories. Surrounding the outside walls of the cylindrical inside are eight smaller arches, whose small concrete looking conclave was resemblement of an empty fireplace but shone brightly with light. At the front of the lobby beneath the centre-point where the stairs met above it was a large ornamental throne, sat in which was an even larger but slightly older looking shadow man who nodded at Thorak as a sign of respect and gratitude for completing his assignment, collecting the boy.

Max stood by Thorak's side, looking towards the throne but not daring to make eye contact with the man who sat in it. Raising his hand towards the ceiling, the man on the throne projecting a small glowing orb into the center of the atrium, it rose slowly and smoothly towards the ceiling before forcefully into the ground below, flames of light spreading out from the center point of impact that stopped just before Max's feet before being sucked back into its point of origin and disappearing leaving no resonance of its existence left. Within seconds each of the eight portways around the atrium lit up as shadow creatures entered in numbers until around thirty others stood before Max, whose face was a picturesque portrayal of both shock and excitement in the realisation that there were more like him than he could have ever contemplated.

"I am Zanthar, king of the shadow realm" Spoke the

large creature rising to his feet from the throne he had previously been sat on, Max nodded locking eyes for the first time with the king who addressed him directly. Max could feel the eyes of the others around him all staring and examining him as he stood like cattle in a market waiting to hear his fate which was clearly now in the hands of those surrounding him. "I know that you will have your questions dear boy, and I will do my best to answer them now" the king spoke his voice soothing yet authoritative "Each of us has been tasked..." he begins, looking around the room so as to address them all "and each of us has been gifted" he continues, pausing momentarily. "We are the guardians of darkness, the protectors of this realm, and have been since time begun!" The king continues raising his voice as he speaks, and those around the room begin to nod and murmur in agreement and pride. "We Max, are the keepers of peace, protectors of our own and together we are not only an unstoppable force, but we are a family!" he pauses once again, ushering silence from the others with his hands. "You have the choice dear boy, you are now one of our species, but do you wish to be one of our kin?" he speaks more softly walking towards Max who stood silent. Stopping just before Max he stood tall towering over the smaller boy, all of the surrounding creatures knelt in honour and respect for their king, leaving Max and him as the only ones standing. Max thought momentarily through everything he had been through, his aloneness, fears, near death experiences, and knew what he truly wanted inside. Dropping to his knees he knelt before the king who then spoke only four words "Welcome to the order!".

Printed in Great Britain
by Amazon